FREE YOURSELF

FREE YOURSELF

S. BREAKER

Zeta Indie Publishing

For my alternate self

Contents

I

Fold

Three days from today

"Well, hell's bells. That was close."

Laney flinched in surprise when she heard the familiar voice. She tried to look around but even as she was sure her eyes were open, she could see nothing but blackness.

Then she heard someone else speak. Someone whose voice she didn't recognize.

"We've got her, Berry."

"Thank goodness."

"What? Who is that?" Lancy rubbed her eyes. She thought she could almost glimpse something, only everything was blurry. She started to heave, feeling the beginnings of panic.

She tried to feel around for Noah since she couldn't hear him coughing to recover from the quantum shear jump as usual. But she could grasp nothing but thin air.

Then Laney heard another voice. Female. With a strange but vaguely familiar cadence.

"AG levels nominal."

Laney felt a sudden but brief wave of nausea and she blinked hard just as her eyesight finally began to focus. She blinked a few more times, trying to gain her bearings.

The dim blue light in the room adjusted slightly to illuminate her surroundings.

"Noah?" she called out. Her throat felt raw. She tried to clear it. Her head snapped up when she heard a short hissing sound and when she looked up, she saw a hazy image of someone.

A big guy with deep brown skin had taken off a pressurized helmet. He was standing a few feet away as he unclipped his hazmat suit, or spacesuit, or something, tucking his helmet under his arm.

"Are you okay?" he asked, his dark eyes looking a bit concerned that she looked like she was about to scramble away in alarm at any moment.

Laney's eyes moved around warily.

A few feet away, metal crates and boxes were stacked in tidy rows, almost as tall as the moderate headroom. Closed locker doors were recessed into the gray panel walls lining both sides of the room. The rest of the place was bare, muted, with a minimal, sterile aesthetic. She could hear muffled thumps from underneath the floor and above her head, and on and off, there was a sort of shushing sound.

She clenched her fists. "Who are you? Where am I? What is this place?"

The over-polished, hollow feel of her surroundings made

Laney think she might be underwater, back in Berry's submarine.

"Hey, Laney," the disembodied voice of Berry came on.

Her eyes lit up. *Berry?*

"Guess where you are."

Hearing Berry's familiar voice again put her at ease and her posture relaxed a touch. She craned her neck to look around and then spotted the window at the far end of the room.

She had to squint to see outside. Then she held her breath in astonishment.

The darkness could have indicated night. There were definitely stars outside.

But there was no mistaking that the bright wispy clusters outside the window weren't simply clouds.

Laney's stomach did a tumble as she realized what the hollow feel of the strange place indicated. "I'm in outer space," she murmured her awed reply.

She glanced back to meet the gaze of the big guy, whom underneath the spacesuit she could see had on a shiny jumpsuit uniform that had a blue spiral logo on the chest and important-looking patches on the sleeve.

"Miss Laney Carter." His smile widened. "Welcome to the Dauntless. We've been expecting you." He held his hand out to help her up. "I'm Dek, the Science officer."

Laney straightened up from the grated metal floor, already heading straight toward the small curved window to marvel at the view, her jaw dropping in wonder at the endless sea of stars set against the blackness of space.

"Where are we exactly?"

Dek paused as if to calculate. "We're still in the Milky Way, about three hundred and fifty light-years from Earth."

"Wow," Laney whispered, her heart pounding in excitement, unable to tear her gaze away from the void.

Despite everything that had already happened to her since discovering the existence of parallel worlds, Laney had never once considered that her path would take her this far out of the planet, not to mention the solar system.

Then again, she hadn't exactly been having a normal last couple of weeks. Nothing that had happened could be further from her average teenage life back in New England.

Dek was watching her with a small smirk. "See something interesting?"

Laney grinned. "Let's just say last year's school trip to the planetarium pales in comparison to the real deal." She looked around eagerly. "Where's Berry? Where's Noah?"

"I'm on the comms, Laney." Berry's tone was reassuring, even as his voice crackled a bit coming over an overhead speaker. "As you've probably inferred, I'm not actually on the ship, or in the dimension."

She blew out a breath. "Oh boy, you have no idea how glad I am to hear your voice. How did you escape The Alliance?" she wanted to know, a sudden urgency creeping into her tone. "What's going on over there?"

Berry's reply sounded somber. "I've been hiding out at Rui's sister's lab in the Pacific Ocean for the last couple of days. They have quite a sophisticated security grid so I've been able to avoid The Alliance." He paused, sounding hesitant. "I'm still waiting to hear about what's happened in the city, but—"

Laney was already making a face.

"Preliminary reports haven't been good," Berry finished.

She furrowed her eyebrows in concern. "Is Maia okay?"

"I'm sorry, Laney. I haven't heard from her yet. I did hear that the University was attacked but don't worry, I'll let you know as soon as I get word."

She nodded in reluctant resignation. There was nothing she could do about the situation in the other parallel world. She had a more important mission to be getting on with and as always, she was running out of time.

Laney cast another look around. "Where's Noah? Did he arrive earlier than me again?"

Dek looked perplexed and Laney thought he looked like he didn't know who she was talking about.

She gave him an expectant questioning look. "Come on. Dr. Noah Donovan," she supplied with a brief waving gesture. "Arrogant ninja spy scientist? Very bad social skills. Broods a lot?"

A shadow fell on Dek's face.

Laney tensed, already feeling dread as she realized the real reason for his pause. "What? Where is he?"

"Berry," Dek called out his suggestion. "Maybe it's better you tell her."

Laney's heart pounded in her chest again. "Tell me. Tell me *now*."

Berry sounded like he took a deep breath before he spilled it. "The Alliance managed to intercept your quantum jump. In fact, they almost got you both. I'm so sorry, Laney."

She swallowed hard, her chest constricting. "Oh my god." She looked up at Dek again. "Is he still alive?" she pressed.

"You know where he is, right? There's some sort of plan. We're on our way to rescue him right now?"

"Um..." Dek's eyebrows rose before he could formulate a response, another female voice came over the PA system and Dek looked up in alert.

"Dek, do you have her?"

Dek tapped the communicator attached to his earlobe. "That's an affirmative, Commander," he replied.

He motioned with his hand as he led the way to the automatic door that slid open. "Listen, why don't I walk you to your quarters to get cleaned up first?" he offered Laney. "Then we can all debrief on the bridge."

"What?" Laney's expression was panicked disbelief. "We don't have time for that. We have to find Noah now!" She bolted out the door, making it down the narrow corridor and around the corner before even realizing she had no idea where she was going.

She stopped short, gasping heavily. "Oh shit." She threw up her hands as she looked around the empty, dimly lit passageway.

She wanted to kick herself for being so rash, but having spent most of the last few days running away from mortal threats, it had become automatic, almost like an impulse.

She stepped tentatively to the left before stopping again, already confused. "How the hell do I get to the bridge?" she mumbled, almost under her breath.

"Take the next left and the upward hatch D-7 to get to the bridge."

"Whoa!" Laney jumped.

It was that odd but vaguely-familiar female voice again,

except Laney couldn't see anyone else around who may have spoken. It was as though the voice was coming from everywhere.

Laney's mouth hung slightly open. "Am I...hallucinating right now?"

"*Please restate your question.*"

She blinked in recognition. *Oh!* Then she asked again if only to try once more, "Computer, how do I get to the bridge?"

"*Take the next left and the upward hatch D-7 to get to the bridge.*"

Laney grinned. "Thanks."

"*Of course.*"

She almost chuckled to herself in relief before whirling around to follow the computer's directions, her footsteps echoing loud thuds on the floor as she ran down the corridor.

Dek turned to look the moment Laney appeared at the top of the stairs. "There she is," was all he said with an amused tone of voice.

Laney's eyes widened as she stepped through the doorway leading to the bridge.

It was smaller than what Star Trek would have you believe, with control panels covering most of the walls, screens, switches, and boards with rows and rows of different-colored little status lights.

There were two vacant seats mounted on the wall behind her and another guy wearing the same jumpsuit uniform as Dek, sitting before what looked like a podium with a control panel to the right, who merely gave her a disinterested glance before returning to work.

Then there was the huge picture window right up front

which offered an incredible view of what was right ahead of and directly above the ship and Laney could only stare in awe at the grand vastness of what lay before them.

She couldn't help but feel so small.

Dek was leaning against another console, a little off-center, monitoring a little screen with blinking dots. The chair he was standing by swiveled around and Laney met the gaze of the young woman with cropped blonde hair and gray eyes sitting in it as she gave Laney a scrutinizing look.

It made Laney feel even smaller.

"Miss Carter," the blonde began with an authoritative tone before she pushed off the chair to approach Laney.

"Uh..." Laney's throat went dry as she braced herself for whatever scolding she was about to receive.

Just then, a tall woman with curly hair, wearing overalls over the same jumpsuit uniform sauntered into the bridge and walked up to approach the big chair. She handed the blonde a square tablet. "Here's that report on the last K-jump, Commander Trin."

"Thanks, Sol."

Sol jerked her thumb in Laney's direction. "Who's this?"

"That's Laney," Dek supplied. "She's the girl Berry mentioned we're supposed to be helping get home."

"Berry." Sol's eyes lit up. "Oh, you mean that guy that comes on the intercom a lot?"

Laney pursed her lips. She was a little bit flummoxed how everyone seemed pretty calm and business as usual when they should be burning all the thrusters or something to save Noah's life ASAP.

"Commander," Laney began to Trin. "I'm so sorry to interrupt but we need to find my friend right now. It's urgent." Her tone was nothing but serious, if not a little bit shaky.

Sol's eyebrows lifted at her directness, but Trin kept reading the report.

Trin's manner was nonchalant. "I'm very sorry about your friend but our agreement with Berry was to help *you* get home," she explained. "We're already risking enough as it is." She shrugged. "Besides, my understanding from Berry is that there's a particular appointment you urgently need to attend. Any deviations from our current course will cause delays."

"No, no, no, no, no." Laney shook her head. "We have to go find Noah. The Alliance has him. He's in terrible danger."

Trin gave the tablet back to Sol then called out to the other guy sitting at the console on the right. "Cam, it looks like we're still getting that residual disruption to the backup systems. Can you run a diagnostic on the ion reactor? The last thing we want right now is a broken jump drive."

"Commander, please," Laney implored. "We have to go. We have to go *now*."

Trin regarded her with a look and a pause. Then she drawled, "Sigrid, can you pull up a map of our course?"

A holographic map flickered up overlaying the main viewing window.

Laney looked taken aback. "Your ship's computer is called Sigrid? As in *Siri*?"

Dek interjected offhand. "She's an advanced evolution of AI from our Earth. Think she was originally used for mobile phones or something."

Laney's eyebrows rose in amusement. It was no wonder her voice sounded so familiar.

Trin studied the map for a second. "We're already more than halfway to our destination," she relayed. "Besides, we'd need to do a trace on all intercepted messages to the fleet to even figure out where they're holding your friend."

"I've already taken the liberty of doing a trace, Commander. Dr. Noah Donovan is on the generation ship Aquila, currently 1.3 light-hours from Earth, near the orbit of Saturn."

Laney blinked in surprise.

Trin pursed her lips knowingly. "Were you eavesdropping again, Sigrid?"

"I'm sorry, Commander. It's been a while since we've had visitors."

Laney's eyes popped out. "The computer eavesdrops?"

Trin shook her head. "She's got quite an attitude. I'm not sure they programmed her correctly."

All of a sudden, a loud alarm blared on the PA, every control panel and status light in sight started blinking red, the sliding door to the bridge shushed closed, and steam or smoke billowed from the air vents in the ceiling.

"Cabin decompression in twenty seconds."

Trin yelled out, "Jeez, Sigrid! I was just kidding. Lighten up."

The alarm instantly turned off and everything turned gray again.

Dek laughed out loud.

Laney wanted to laugh too if she hadn't nearly thrown up in a panic. After everything she'd been through, the absolute last thing she could take was to almost suffocate in the vacuum of space.

"So dramatic." Trin rolled her eyes. "Either way, The

Aquila sounds like it's three hundred and fifty light-years in the wrong direction. Besides, wasn't this guy a soldier? He would have known the risks. He knew what he was getting himself into."

"No!" Laney clenched her fists in indignation. "That's not an option! We have to save him. We can't just leave him there. *I'm* not just going to leave him there."

Trin gave her an even look. "You realize you're risking your only way to get back to your homeworld. You understand that, right?"

Sol had stepped back beside Cam's station, her arms crossed over her chest.

"What are you doing?" he asked, looking up at her briefly as he worked.

"Watching a battle of wills," Sol quipped. "When was the last time anyone stood up to the Commander like this? Feel like we need some popcorn."

Dek's shoulders shook in mirth but he didn't comment.

Cam raised his hand, regarding them all with a look. "For the record, I signed on to this mission to explore deep space, not to put my entire career on the line to commit inter-dimensional treason." Then his tone changed. "But if you're all keen, I'm good to go." He met Trin's narrow-eyed gaze and shrugged. "Just sayin'."

Sol chuckled again.

"Dek?" Trin prompted after a moment.

Dek spoke softly. "If he was one of us, you know as well as I do, we would never leave him behind."

Trin tilted her head in deep thought as if letting his words sink in.

Laney watched the exchange, looking from one of them to the other.

Dek and Trin were facing in opposite directions at an angle, not even touching, not even looking at each other, but anyone would already be able to tell there was something between the two of them. It was as though their entire posture and body language changed the moment the other drew near.

"Oh my god," Laney exclaimed in realization. "You guys are primaries."

Trin raised an eyebrow at her. "You know about primaries?"

Dek glanced up from his console.

Laney blinked as if to snap out of a trance. "I mean—I've just heard the theory. It *is* only a theory though. Right?" There was an oddly urgent catch in her tone.

Dek raised his eyebrows as if to consider it. "It's open to interpretation, but I would say it's pretty solid as far as theories go."

Trin shot her a look. "You two are too, aren't you? You and this Noah."

Laney stiffened nervously. "Um, I don't know. Sort of, I guess."

"You don't know?" Trin looked amused. "Honey, I think you missed the point. You are primaries *because you know*."

Laney made a face. "It's complicated."

Trin put her hands up in resignation. "Sure, if you say so."

Then she cast a glance around the bridge, put her hands to her hips, then blew out a huge breath. "Alright," she decided with a nod. "What the hell."

Sol put her palms up. "Hold up. So we're seriously doing this?"

Trin gave her a slight shrug. "You'd better get back to Engineering."

"Hah." Sol let out a laugh. "Girl, you're crazier than I thought." Then she grinned. "I like it," she declared before whirling around to exit the bridge, the door closing behind her.

Laney met Trin's gaze again and there was no disguising the relief or gratitude on her face. "Thank you. Thank you so much."

Trin merely cracked a smirk and gave her a wink. "Let's buckle up!" she announced as she hopped into her chair at the same time as she whirled it around to face forward.

Dek motioned Laney to one of the seats near the back. "Make sure you're strapped in," he said, moving to show her how to put the seatbelt on. "You might feel a bit dizzy for a sec. We'll have to disable the artificial gravity again to power up the K-drive."

"The K-drive?" Laney narrowed her eyes in curiosity as she clipped the five-point safety harness around her.

"The Kennedy drive," Dek answered. "The Dauntless is a prototype. This is the first ship in the fleet to successfully achieve space folding."

"All the other ships can only do sublight speeds so far, including The Aquila," Trin stated, sounding proud of the fact.

"The tech is remarkably similar to your quantum shear technology as it's also based on black hole principles," Dek went on even as he strapped himself into his own chair. "I can tell you more about it later on."

"Attention," Trin pressed a button on her communicator and her voice came over the PA. "All hands. Prepare for zero-G." Then she looked over and gave a nod to Cam who flipped the switch.

"Artificial gravity disabled."

Laney held her breath, and as soon as Sigrid made her announcement, she felt her arms begin to drift up that she was sure if she wasn't belted down into her seat, she would be floating around the room.

Her stomach stirred in slight nausea but she clenched her jaw in determination. *Hold on, Noah,* she thought fervently. *I'm coming.*

"Cam, set a course for the generation ship Aquila," Trin ordered.

"Aye."

"Engaging the K-Drive," Dek announced, flipping several switches.

"Space jump in 3, 2, 1..."

2

First

Eighteen months ago

Laney could see her breath as white puffs in the cold as she ran toward her friend who was waiting at the top of the bleachers.

Darla threw up her hands as she spotted her. "Finally!" She rubbed her hands together to keep warm as she gave Laney coming closer a pointed look. "I swear to god, Laney Carter," she started. "If you manage to ever be on time for anything, I will die of actual shock," she spoke, already turning to head down the stadium steps to find a seat among the noisy, colorful crowd of New England ice hockey fans, all decked out in blue and white, waving flags and foam fingers.

"Whatever, Darla," Laney dismissed. "You're just always early."

Darla gestured to the time on the giant scoreboard

mounted above the rink as she walked. "Uh hello? Technically, you are exactly thirteen minutes and forty-five seconds late to the final game of the season."

Laney laughed. "I didn't realize you were this crazy about school sports."

"Oh come on, this is the last social event before summer break. I wouldn't miss it."

"And it looks like everyone else had the same notion," Laney mused as she looked around the seats packed with students.

"I know, right? Was campus empty?" Darla wanted to know.

"Yup." Laney nodded, rubbing her own hands together. "Total ghost town."

"Yesss," Darla breathed in triumph as they found some empty seats right by the aisle. "Hey guys, could you squeeze down a bit, please?" She motioned to the other students sitting in the row to make space. "Thanks. Hey." She nudged Laney as they settled into their seats. "What was that you were trying to tell me before fifth period today?"

"Oh. That."

"Yeah. Sorry." She shook her head. "Julian was being heinous about the school band try-outs. It's like he thinks we don't have another whole year of this, you know? And of course, his problems supersede anyone else's."

Laney hesitated.

Darla studied her expression. "What is it?" she asked, already sounding suspicious.

"Remember I told you I had that dream—"

"Yes, the one with Mr. Hotness, of course," Darla interjected, already nodding.

Laney laughed at her quick response.

"What?" Darla put her hands up innocently.

Laney opened her mouth to speak but her next statement was interrupted by a rally on the ice and she and Darla looked over.

A broad-shouldered hockey player on their home team had done an intercept, going for a breakaway, and was fielding the puck down the rink. He called out to a teammate, doing an effortless pass, before the next guy neatly thwacked the puck into the net for a goal, making the entire stadium practically shake in celebration.

"YES!" Darla stood up, clapping her hands, to cheer out loud with the crowd.

Laney made a face, waiting for the cheers to die down and for Darla to settle back in her seat before she went on with her story. "So I had the dream again," she told Darla.

"Sweetie, we've all been there. I mean, look at the guy." Darla gestured toward the game.

Laney looked over at the rink again.

Both teams had been called back to the bench.

The hockey player with the broad shoulders made a smooth sliding stop right near the glass before skating over to join the rest of his team in their huddle to receive directions on the next play.

He stood among his teammates with a confident stance, looking intense, looking like he knew exactly what he was doing, like he knew he absolutely belonged in the hockey rink, as though he owned it.

Mr. Hotness.

Jake Donovan.

Jake was a popular campus figure, captain of the hockey team, quite a guy with the females from what Laney had heard, but they'd hardly ever crossed paths. They'd never had to. She didn't even think he knew her name.

Jake took off his helmet, and with the end of the first period, Laney noticed his skin was shiny with sweat, and his usually slicked-back black hair was all tousled and unruly. She narrowed her eyes in a vague recall of the weird dream that was already beginning its slow fade into oblivion in the recesses of her brain.

Darla's eyebrows rose as she watched Laney's expression. "I'm sorry. I'm missing what could possibly be wrong with having this dream?"

Laney fidgeted. "It's...weird. Isn't it?"

"Well." Darla shrugged. "Maybe it's a sign that, you know, you should ask him out."

Laney burst out laughing. "What? Come on, be serious."

"What? I think that would be awesome!"

Laney's jaw dropped a little, giving her friend a look like she'd forgotten how things worked in the real world. "He's absolutely out of my league," she pointed out. "He doesn't even know I exist. That would be like a...frog asking out an eagle."

Darla shot her a look. "That is a horrible metaphor," she remarked. "So what did you want me to say then? Clearly, you were already expecting a certain response."

"I'm saying this is the third time it's happened in the last few weeks, and I was asking you more for like, dream interpretation stuff," Laney explained. "It's symbolic. It has to be," she argued.

Darla pursed her lips. "Girl, you've known me for six

years. What on earth makes you think I know anything about dream interpretation? I am a musician," she enunciated. "Not a psychotherapist." She thought it over. "Why don't you ask one of those ones your parents keep on retainer for their legal cases?"

Laney looked at her like the answer was perfectly obvious. "Because it's a stupid question." She cringed. "And I don't want some stranger picking my brains trying to figure out the underlying meaning of some random dream."

"Fine. Have it your way." Darla sighed. "So, this dream of yours with Jake Donovan, tell me, are you two like, making out like crazy in it? 'Cause, sister, please, I would totally be on that like, well, me on him," she suggested, wiggling her eyebrows.

Laney shook her head in mirth. "Darla," she chided. "Of course we weren't. I think we were just talking or something. Or we were working on a project together...something like that." She waved dismissively, unable to recall any clearer.

"Oh yeah, working on getting it on!" Darla started dancing in her seat. "Man, if only I could have your dreams."

Laney laughed and turned her attention to the Zamboni cleaning the ice.

Darla elbowed Laney again, her eyes glued to someone else sitting in their row, or more accurately, someone else's snacks. "Ooh, look. They have chili fries today," she noted.

"Didn't you eat after band practice?"

"Not chili fries."

Laney gave her an amused look as Darla was looking at her expectantly. "Something on my face? Or is that you assuming that I'm the one who's going to go get the food?"

"Hey, you're the one that took forever to get here." Darla shot her a stubborn look, motioning for her to go.

Laney chuckled, then she sighed in defeat. "Fine."

As Darla stood up in the aisle to let Laney move past, she happened to look up over Laney's shoulder and her eyes lit up. "Oh, hey, Thomas!"

Laney glanced over and recognized their friend from the debate team. She gave him a short nod in greeting.

"Hey—" Thomas did a double-take when he met her gaze. "Laney?" He looked surprised as he came up to them. "How did you get here so fast?"

Laney shot him a look. "What are you talking about?"

Thomas looked puzzled as he gestured aimlessly behind him. "I thought I just saw you at the walkway by the gym on the other side of campus."

"What?" Laney wrinkled her nose.

Thomas tilted his head. "I could've sworn it was you," he said. "I thought you even waved hello at me. I mean, I wanted to ask what you were doing with those weird orange cones, but you seemed to be busy, so I thought I'd leave you to it."

Darla and Laney exchanged looks then Darla peered up at Thomas. "Orange cones? You feeling okay, Tom?"

Laney gave him a look. "Tom, I've been here with Darla since 'Go' time."

"—thirteen minutes and forty-five seconds past 'Go' time," Darla interjected.

"—thank you, Darla," Laney quipped dryly before continuing to Thomas. "Either way, I was here."

"Whatever. Never mind then," Thomas dismissed with a wave as he moved around to stand beside Darla. "I must have been seeing things. Wouldn't be the first time," he added with a laugh.

"I'll bet," Darla said knowingly and she and Laney laughed.

"Oh, there he is," Thomas piped up as he looked up past Laney's head.

Laney turned toward where he was looking and spotted the cute blonde guy walking up toward them. He was carrying two popcorn boxes and big soda cups in a carton in one hand, and a heaped cardboard plate of chili fries in the other.

"Hey Tom," the blonde guy greeted with a small wave.

"Hey," Thomas replied, before gesturing to Laney and Darla. "You guys know my man Kevin, right?"

Darla's forehead was creased. "Whitfield?" she prompted before nodding. "I think we had World History together last year."

Kevin's eyes lit up in recognition. "I think you're right. Darla, isn't it?" he guessed with a smile before his gaze settled on Laney. "And...?"

"Eleanor Carter," Darla supplied before Laney whacked her arm.

"*Laney*. It's *Laney*—Carter," Laney corrected pointedly. "Nobody really calls me Eleanor."

That made Kevin laugh. "Alright then," he replied with a nod. "It's nice to properly meet you, Laney Carter."

"Likewise."

A loud cheer rocked the stadium as the second period of the game started.

"Hey, you guys want to join us to watch the rest of the game?" Darla offered, even as she openly eyed the plate of fries that Kevin was holding.

"Sounds great," Kevin replied with a chuckle, glancing over to give Laney an enchanted look.

And she smiled.

3

Again

Today

"So let me get this straight." Rui shot Laney a no-nonsense, slightly incredulous look.

"You've only arrived in this world five days ago. And already, you've been chased down the street, had your life threatened twice, offended the President and Prime minister, recovered lost memories, been kidnapped by some bad guys, almost got killed by some god-awful machine, and spent nearly an entire day in the hospital to recover?"

Laney looked up from her half-eaten plate of waffles to give Rui's prompting gaze a straightforward look. "Sounds terrible when you put it that way."

"Well, technically," Maia interjected, holding her own fork up to make her point. "The bad guys didn't kidnap Laney.

They just brain-jacked her to get her to walk over to their HQ on her own."

"*Aaand* now it sounds worse," Laney quipped.

Rui was still staring at her. "And now you're what? Waiting here at the dockside café for Dr. Vermillion's submarine to arrive from Geneva so that you can go ahead and put your life at risk all over again? Man, you're brave."

Laney tilted her head. "Brave? No. Stuck? Yes." She gave Rui a once-over and gestured to the several bags hanging off her shoulders, rolling suitcase on the floor by her feet, ticket in her hand. "Are you going to miss your flight?"

Rui snapped to attention almost in a panic, squinting up in the setting sun's glare to see through the giant skylight windows of the red brick building that served as the hub for the ships that arrived at and departed from the capital city, but she was put at ease upon sighting the top of the huge airship that was still docked at the waterfront.

"I'm sure I have a few more minutes," she said, shaking her head. "I'm almost sorry I have to go back to Singapore this evening. I would have wanted to stick around and see what else would go down. As you might have guessed, not much happens in our biosphere laboratory." Her face brightened. "This is all so exciting and *you* are seriously amazing!"

Laney put her hands up. "Hey, but you're talking about it like I'm doing everything on my own." She gestured beside her. "Maia was the neuroscience expert who helped me recover my memories."

"You're welcome, by the way," Maia mumbled through her mouthful of food.

Laney went on, gesturing behind her. "And Noah's been

burdened with the unfortunate task of keeping me alive, which as it turns out?" She wrinkled her nose in bitterness. "Not as straightforward as one would think."

The three of them looked up across the platform, toward the open deck that wrapped around the façade of the building, where a tall, broad-shouldered guy was leaning against the balcony, a guarded expression on his face as he kept a lookout for the sub.

"Wow, the brilliant Dr. Noah Donovan," Rui said almost reverently. "I mean, I'd heard about him—about as much as I'd heard about you, but I had no idea he was so *hot*," she remarked, her voice lowering on her last statement.

Laney began to let out an exasperated sigh. "He's not *that*—"

Maia cleared her throat pointedly, loudly.

Laney stopped and rolled her eyes.

One of the things that Laney had learned so far about interdimensional travel was that often, nothing was what it seemed. Certain people, she'd discovered, could even go as far as to look completely different and yet still potentially be the same.

Dr. Maia Chambers was a case in point, as, to Laney, she felt like she was her oldest best friend from her own world. Even though Laney was pretty sure that there was no way her redheaded friend Darla Addleton would ever get away with Maia's dark alt makeup, twisted high ponytail, and the shell tattoo she sported on her collarbone.

On the other hand, despite the resemblance between Noah and Jake Donovan being incredibly uncanny, there was absolutely no denying that Noah was a hundred percent *not* Jake Donovan.

With his heavy flight jacket over a pair of worn, faded jeans, instead of preppy jock clothes, not to mention the hair, it wouldn't take more than a few seconds to tell them apart on the outside.

Jake Donovan was a popular, chatty, arrogant, probably spoiled, but otherwise normal teenager. Whereas Noah had forgotten even the mere basics of social conventions. He had absolutely no idea how to deal with other people. He was unfriendly, standoffish, and then there was the constant brooding, which Laney figured probably came with the Special Forces training and having grown up in this particular alternate world.

He's a good kisser though.

Laney blinked quickly to halt that train of thought, even as her stomach already fluttered in the recall of certain still-vivid memories. She scolded herself. She wanted to blame Eleanor again—*their* Laney. These weren't really her own feelings. She was convinced that these had been just Noah's late fiancée's feelings bleeding through her. They had to be.

And given what Laney had discovered that Noah might have a connection with the people who had tried to erase her, needless to say, whatever she was feeling and whoever's feelings they were, one thing was clear.

Noah was off-limits.

Maia was still looking at her expectantly.

"Alright, fine." Laney threw up her hands in resignation. "He's totally hot. But you know what? He's super unfriendly and rude and sneaky and deceptive."

Maia and Rui laughed.

Noah glanced over as though sensing that the girls were talking about him, but he only met Laney's gaze briefly before turning back to look out the water.

"Whatever. Props, man." Rui put her hand up to give Laney a high-five. "I'm pretty sure I wouldn't have half the stones to deal with whatever all that is you're dealing with right now."

Laney chuckled and obliged.

"So would you like to join us?" Maia motioned to Rui. "Laney's ordered enough food here to feed a battalion."

"Yeah, they serve waffles *all day* here," Laney informed her, her eyes almost scandalous.

Rui gave her a curious look as though it was a well-known fact. "Um, of course they do?" She noted the table covered with what looked like every kind of brunch food in the world and laughed again. "What, you don't have food in your world?"

"Not for free we don't," Laney quipped as she reached for another pastry from across the table. "And I can't believe you guys have cronuts here, too! Seriously, I'm in heaven right now."

Just then, a flying drone zipped over carrying another box of food which it effortlessly deployed onto the last empty spot on the table.

"Oh," Laney murmured in delight. "Food delivery by drone. I love it," she said, already reaching into the box of pastries to direct an entire profiterole straight into her mouth.

Maia watched her, amused. "Tell me again about this tired notion of 'home' you have and why you can't just quit while you're ahead—*nay*, alive," she pointed out. "And stay in our awesome world with us?" She leaned back then paused as if feeling the need to qualify. "World-wiping, apocalyptic cascade bomb *aside*. Which technically *was* over sixty years ago."

Laney's chewing slowed as she looked around.

If she didn't already know that more than ninety-five percent of the rest of the world lay in ruins, she wouldn't be able to tell from where she was sitting.

From across the balcony, on the horizon, she could see a couple of airships hovering in the burnt orange sky above the darkening blue harbor surrounded by rolling green hills, dotted with quaint bungalow houses; the backdrop for the contrasting combination of new and also well-preserved colonial structures of the cozy central business district that still sparkled in what was left of the daylight.

It really was beautiful.

She'd be lying if she said she hadn't thought about it.

Laney sighed as she turned back to Maia. "I think you're forgetting a certain group of people who've already tried to kill me once before, who've also promised to try again for as long as I remained here."

"Yeah, yeah. The Alliance," Maia supplied, offhand.

Rui's eyes popped open in shock. "*Maji de?*"

Laney smacked Maia's arm.

"Ow!" Maia yelped.

Laney gave Maia a pointed look. "Nothing. Nobody." She waved her hand to dismiss it.

The Alliance was a secret organization whose mission was to safeguard science—but only the science that *they* deemed acceptable. And unfortunately, Laney with her weird extra-dimensional condition had not made the cut.

The people in this world only believed the organization to be a myth. And even though Laney obviously knew otherwise, divulging of or confirming their existence was totally forbidden. But after only having met Maia five days ago, she'd already found out that Maia was terrible at keeping secrets.

Maia made a face, rubbing her arm before she reached for some more food.

Laney gave Rui a sheepish smile. "Sorry about that."

But Rui grinned. "Hey, I understand. In the plant world, we have secrets too," she teased with a wink. "Did you know that the coneflower, more commonly known as Echinacea, is said to have amazing healing properties?" She paused, pursing her lips. "Well, I guess that's not so much of a secret."

They both laughed.

"Can I just say I think it's amazing that you've maintained speaking your native Japanese in your family," Maia noted to Rui, even as she was concentrated on picking out the sprinkles from her donut to eat them first. "It's such a shame that some of these beautiful cultures are lost forever."

"Hey, maybe Laney can teach you to speak Japanese too," Rui suggested with a confident nod.

Maia was trying to keep a straight face. "Right."

Laney fidgeted in her seat, not willing to get into that any further, and instead, changed the subject. "Hey, so, pull up a chair." With her toe, she nudged one of the chairs out from under the table for Rui.

"It's alright. Simon from my team should be by soon to—oh, there he is."

Laney and Maia looked over to see both Simon and Kevin walking over to them. Simon's gaze seemed to be distracted off to one side. Kevin's hand was already raised in greeting.

"Hi girls," Kevin greeted with a smile as the two of them came up to the café.

"Hey, Kevin," Laney replied then she looked over at Simon. "Hey Simon, how's it going? Are you guys leaving today too?"

Simon cast her a wary look and his smile looked forced. "Hi. Laney." He glanced up sideways furtively and Laney realized he was trying to watch out for Noah from across the platform as though making sure he wouldn't see him.

Laney watched Simon curiously, but Rui spoke before she could press on.

"I think we haven't met yet," Rui said, putting her hand out for Kevin to shake. "I'm Rui Minato."

"Oh." Laney's eyes lit up. "This is Kevin Whitfield, my b—" *Boyfriend!* she was about to say. She faked a loud cough to cover her slip. She wanted to kick herself. Not *this* Kevin! "Oh, wow." She mocked slapping her chest to clear her throat. "Those pastries are a total choking hazard."

Maia didn't even flinch. She slid a glass of water across the table which Laney immediately grabbed and bottomed up.

But Kevin just grinned and looked over at Rui, extending his hand. "Kevin Whitfield. Nice to meet you."

Rui nodded. "Likewise."

"Kevin's joining our team for a few weeks," Simon explained, still fidgeting in his stance. "He'll be going to Singapore with us to help study the southern *rata*."

"It was endemic to this region before the cascade bomb," Kevin informed Laney. "We thought it was extinct but somehow there have been new sightings of it up near the equatorial territories. We're hoping to bring back some samples of it to see if it thrives again in temperate conditions."

"Isn't that amazing," Maia remarked. "What a stubborn little plant. It must have somehow adapted through the years to be able to grow outside its usual climate, against all odds."

"Yes, and if we can determine how it's evolved this way, we might possibly be able to apply the process to re-cultivate other plant species that were lost," Simon explained with a small shrug.

"Not to mention its implications on our efforts on genetics research in general," Maia put in, her eyes bright.

Kevin chuckled as he recognized the look in Maia's eyes. "Someone stop her before she starts quoting from her world-famous paper again."

"What? I'm just saying the breakthroughs to be made in this area of study are infinite and the potential impact could be global," Maia argued.

"That's right though!" Simon spoke up then he winced slightly as though he hadn't meant to sound so excited. "I mean," he went on, his voice lowered. "We're only barely scratching the surface here, but if we're even a small percentage successful, it'll already be worth the shot."

"It'll certainly be a great step toward regenerating our world," Rui said with an eager nod.

"See?" Maia prompted Kevin with a self-satisfied look. "That's what I meant."

Kevin simply shook his head in mirth.

Then Maia noticed Laney's bored expression. "Hey, Laney,"

she said, elbowing her. "What does Rui's team do again?" she asked, her tone teasing.

Laney gave her a flat look then she put a finger up. "They're dendrological geneticists," she said, emphasizing her enunciation.

Rui winked at her. "You got it!"

"Oh, whatever," Laney dismissed, curling her lips. "You guys are all world-renowned accomplished scientists and I'm just the dumbest girl here who almost failed her Chemistry mid-term."

A loud, deep foghorn blast reverberated throughout the departure lobby and they all looked up to attention. The airship was signaling its imminent departure and calling for passengers.

Rui shrugged. "That's us."

Kevin moved to help Rui carry some of her bags.

"It's a shame you guys can't stay for the holidays," Maia said. "Laney said you've only just arrived too."

Simon shook his head. "We've left some time-sensitive experiments back in our lab."

"I can't even imagine," Laney commented in wonder. "The commute back and forth must be a killer, huh?" she prompted Simon but he seemed intent on not meeting her gaze.

Rui replied instead, "We're used to it. And we're very rarely required to come back to The Community anyway." She looked around the group. "Anyone here will tell you, their lab is basically their home."

Laney noted the nods from everyone. "I see."

"I mean my sister and her husband are marine biologists.

They spend most of their time in *their* underwater lab in the middle of the Pacific Ocean," Rui relayed.

"Hey, we'd better go before that flight leaves without us," Simon urged Rui, and Laney noticed him toss another cautious glance toward the balcony.

Rui nodded. "Right. Good luck, Laney. Seriously," she bid with a meaningful look as she pulled on her suitcase. "See you guys later."

"Bye Rui! Bye Simon!" Laney waved.

Simon merely nodded shortly in acknowledgment before he turned to leave.

Then Laney felt Kevin's hand on her shoulder.

"I'll see you around, Laney," he said, smiling at her.

Laney flushed slightly as she met his gaze. "Yeah." She watched as the three of them crossed the lobby headed toward the departure gate, leading up to the ramp going onto the airship.

"Did you notice that?" Laney prompted Maia after a moment.

"What? Kevin's *come hither* look?"

Laney rolled her eyes again. "No," she said. "Simon. It was like he couldn't wait to get away from here. Or *me*."

Maia waved it away.

"You know, it wasn't just him. Even your lab assistant Tak and that Nivan guy from the horticulture lab at the University garden. They were both trying to avoid me this afternoon," she remembered, narrowing her eyes, before giving Maia a questioning look. "Did you say something to them? Are people afraid of me?" But then she reconsidered. "Hang on. It can't be that. I know Rui's not afraid of me. What is it then?"

"Um..." Maia trailed off, her gaze distracting above her shoulder.

Laney turned to look to see Noah only a few yards away.

His expression was serious as always and his voice carried no hint of humor as he relayed to the two of them, "The sub's in the harbor."

Laney's eyes lit up and she looked toward the balcony. "Berry."

4

Sub

"Watch your head," Noah spoke to no one in particular as he stood by the airlock opening as a cue for Maia and Laney to descend the stairs into the belly of the submarine

Laney prepared to duck while holding on to the handrail, but as she moved, she noticed quite a few people gathered up on the viewing deck at the terminal building, all watching them with interest.

It must have been an impressive sight, she figured, even if all they could see was the stylized metal platform upon which the airlock opening was fixed, bobbing slightly above the choppy water. It gave no indication of the sheer size of the giant sub that was a mere dark shadow right beneath the surface.

Noah noticed her gaze wander and followed it. "It's not often that they see a submarine dock here in the city," he explained as he moved to follow behind her.

But instead of responding, Laney walked faster.

She could count on one hand the number of conversations the two of them had had in the last twenty-four hours, which was easily explained since Laney had been doing her absolute best to avoid him.

The tiny nagging suspicion in the back of her mind about Noah had grown in the last day and it was almost enough to choke her.

Obviously, she was grateful to him for saving her life. Again. But she couldn't ignore the facts.

Noah hadn't done much else except to lie to her since the first time they'd met. He had been in league with the government organization that eight months ago had tried to wipe out the entire multiverse, who had also attempted to kill her.

And she'd just found out that Noah was part of The Alliance as well.

That Donovan is such a master of deception...

Laney couldn't figure exactly whose side he was actually on.

Or maybe it was all simpler than she thought.

Noah had made it no great secret right from the beginning what his mission—his *only* mission—was. In fact, the last time they were both in the submarine was before they went on the mission to save Eleanor, only to, unfortunately, end up still losing her anyway.

Laney couldn't even imagine how distraught he must have been—must still be. To have lost his great love, the infamous Nobel Laureate Dr. Eleanor Carter, and yet have an exact replica of her walking about in Laney.

And perhaps he was just waiting for the right time. He

kept saving her life so he could trade her off at the next most profitable opportunity. The greatest bargaining chip ever.

Either way, whatever was going on with Noah, Laney knew none of it was about her. Not really. She was just an obstacle that needed to be got out of the way. And the sooner that they sent her home, so much the better.

Laney squinted as her eyesight adjusted to the dimmer lamps that lit the inside of the submarine.

A guy with spiky wheat blonde hair, glasses, and a holey maroon sweater was standing near the bottom of the winding staircase. "Hi guys!" he greeted them.

"Berry! You made it!" Laney exclaimed.

Berry met her gaze. "So?" He spread his arms out to gesture to their surroundings. "What do you think?"

Laney looked around as fragments of memories came back to her.

The rounded front of the large metal capsule had a railing that ran along the grated floor-to-ceiling windows that looked so thick they had a magnifying effect. Wavy sparkles of light shone in different patterns across the walls and the floors. There were large machines with analog readouts and dials, different colored bulbs blinking from multiple panels, monitoring, and navigational equipment. A handful of strange little creatures were moving around on the floor, their metal bodies bare, gears and spokes poking out of places, running on little treads or wheels.

"It looks—" *the same*, she was about to say.

She stopped short at the last step of the stairs as her gaze fell upon an elevated flat platform table in the center of the main compartment. It had a large peanut-shaped holographic lattice floating above, with different-sized dots glowing over certain points across it.

One of the numerous white-coated lab assistants bustling about the table waved his hand and the hologram enlarged. He touched a point seemingly in mid-air, which made the entire image whoosh away, to be replaced by about a dozen little screens that to Laney looked like CCTV feeds.

"Wow," Laney breathed as she walked past Berry to approach the table.

Maia was already there. She whistled as she appraised the holographic image. "Pretty impressive, Dr. Vermillion."

"This is absolutely fascinating," Laney remarked, turning back to Berry as he came up to her.

"I know, right? We've been working on it for—"

Laney peered closely at him and poked his cheek with her finger. "Boop!"

"What the heck are you doing?" He shot her a strange look.

She grinned. "Just checking that you're not an AI robot," she said, even though she knew full well that Berry's AI robot clone invention had been put away in storage back in Maia's lab at the University after its power source was damaged during Laney's rescue from The Alliance.

"Oh, haha."

"It's really good to see you."

"Likewise."

"Speaking of damaged robots," Maia spoke up as she walked up to Berry to hand him a box of what looked like broken metal scraps.

Laney frowned. "I'm so sorry about P.T.," she began. "I still really feel bad about what happened."

Berry gave her an earnest look. "Look, the little guy helped save your life. That was completely above and beyond what I had designed it to do. So at least you can't say he didn't go out swinging."

Maia patted her back. "Don't worry, Laney. I'm sure Berry can fix it. Berry can fix anything, right?"

He winked at her. "Hey, if I can recover approximately sixty-four percent so far of the Quantum Jump Project's data after it was destroyed last year, I think fixing a little robot will be as easy as *Pi*." He winked, grinning at her then bent down to hand the box to another little robot that in turn wheeled away across the floor and out a compartment door.

Laney gave him an amused look. "So is that what all this is?" she asked, tilting her head in the direction of the holographic lattice.

"Isn't it beautiful?" Berry looked proud. "Big Boss Eleanor and I only used to have a smaller, handwritten version. This is a bit more comprehensive." He waved his hands in the air in a declaration. "I'm calling it 'The Map'—" He paused. "Or 'The Verse'." He paused again. "Or 'The Brane.'" He paused yet again to shake his head briskly. "Still working on the name," he amended.

"A brain? It looks like a peanut." Laney tilted her head to look again.

"No," he corrected. "A brane, like dimensional membranes."

"You've mapped *all* the dimensions in the multiverse?" Maia looked impressed.

"Of course not." Berry made a skeptical face. "We don't have nearly that much data storage. This was just the sample population of what was part of the Quantum Jump Project last year."

"These look like surveillance," Laney said, pointing at the little holographic screens on 'The Map.'

"Oh, the feed is not live. We can't do that. Not yet anyway. These are just clips of what we'd collected during some of the investigations last year."

"Still, this is all pretty cool, Berry." Maia patted his back. "I think another Nobel prize will be in order, and this time you won't have just been Dr. Eleanor Carter's assistant."

Noah was already at a console, manipulating the lattice. His eyes narrowed as he zoomed in and out of several dark patches that looked to appear randomly across the map.

Berry noticed. "Uh, yeah, those are the bits that we haven't fully reconstructed. I'm expecting at least twenty-five percent of the entire data set will be too corrupted to recover."

"Tell me the government is not asking you to restart the project. Tell me that's not why you've done all this." Noah's manner was bone-dry.

"No way!" Berry waved his hands. "They should know better than that by now. Besides, I don't think our world can afford another globally-catastrophic event. No." He shook his head. "This is just for analysis. I mean, we've got tons of data already, enough for my team to study for five years." He shoved his hands in his pockets. "As far as the government is concerned, the breakthrough's already been completed. Any-thing more is a risk they're not willing to take." He looked over at Laney. "GNR has been assigned to take point on this," he noted of their main lab, Global Nuclear Research. "And

I have a mandate to use any resources to facilitate restoring Laney to her original world."

"And I'm sure they can't wait to get rid of me," Laney piped up, recalling that she hadn't exactly left a very good impression with the President and Prime minister.

"Aw." Maia gave her a sympathetic look. "Give them a chance. Maybe they'll warm up to you eventually."

"Not planning on staying here for that long, Maia," Laney reminded her. Then she thumped on Berry's back. "Okay so, what now? We go find that 'supernova' you were talking about?" She gestured air quotes for the word in mocking.

"Supernova?" Maia repeated, looking surprised. "You didn't tell me about that."

"Oh." Laney blinked. "Remember that universal translator thing I was doing—"

"Right, you could speak to anyone in any foreign language it seemed, even obsolete ones."

"Yeah, we found out that that was just a side effect of my...condition," Laney phrased carefully. "The thing is, your illustrious Dr. Carter had given me something." Her gaze slid over to Noah's cautiously, but for a change, he didn't seem incensed to defend Eleanor's good name.

He just met her gaze without a word.

Laney looked away, a slight furrow in her eyebrows. She couldn't quite pin it down, but lately, she sensed that something had changed with Noah. Only it was even more disconcerting than normal.

Berry went on when she paused. "Call it interdimensional insulation," he enunciated. "An especially formulated dose of exotic particles. Basically, it made Laney a tracking point of origin. She served as a reference point. Like on a map, you can't give directions unless you have somewhere to start. It was brilliant because it's what made discovering all the other quantum worlds possible."

"Brilliant," Laney echoed with a wry tone.

"But *horrible*," Berry amended with an instant frown. "Of course. Very, very horrible."

Maia chuckled.

"Yes. Anyway," Laney dismissed. "If I don't get all this stuff out of me, well, let's just say that's where the story ends. I'm not going home. I'm not staying here. I'm not going to...*be*." She made a face. "And apparently, according to Berry, only a supernova blast can effectively *reset* me."

"In theory."

Laney turned an exasperated look over at Berry. "Thanks for that."

"Um, I don't mean to ask the stupid question but wouldn't exposure to a supernova oh say, kill you?" Maia's expression was comical.

"Not the way we're going to do it," Berry quipped confidently.

Noah was busy with the map again. He waved his hand and the peanut lattice dissolved away to be replaced by a holographic diagram of the solar system. He went on to gesture some more and the view panned out three times, then he touched a point in the holographic image and one of the billion stars in the galaxy map blinked and magnified. "Betelgeuse."

An inordinate amount of lists, statistics, and graphs scrolled rapidly down on the screen. But after a moment,

Noah frowned and he consulted the glowing holographic update display (HUD) that activated on his left forearm. "I'm not reading any indications with this star. It looks stable. Are you sure this is the one you meant?"

"Oh." Berry looked hesitant. "See, well, actually, I didn't tell you the other part."

Laney tilted her head. "Why am I not surprised?" she drawled.

"When I said I'd detected an impending supernova in the galaxy," Berry began. "I never said I'd found it in this dimension."

Maia looked taken aback.

But Noah's eyes cleared in understanding.

Laney scoffed. "So this alleged supernova of yours is actually from yet another parallel univ—?" She threw up her hands, almost nonchalantly. "You know what? Sure. Whatever. At this point, I don't know if anything can still shock me anymore."

Berry pursed his lips. "Really? Try this."

"What is that?" Laney peered at the small round device in Berry's hand.

"This." Berry gave her a meaningful, even ceremonious, look. "Is a Zeta device."

5

Traversal

"An *actual* Zeta device."

Laney gasped. "Hell's bells, Berry, you did it!"

Berry looked over at Noah. "This was the main reason I wanted to recover all the project's records. Sorry I didn't tell you, man, but it was necessary."

Noah dismissed it curtly. "It doesn't matter now."

Berry's forehead creased, looking slightly puzzled, but he went on. "And fortunately, when Eleanor made a 'bleed through' the other day and took over Laney's personality, part of the transdimensional formula we cooked up to fix Laney's memory loss was incidentally also the last piece of the puzzle we needed to complete the Zeta device."

"That's brilliant!" Laney shook Berry's shoulder in excitement.

"Congrats, Berry," Maia said. "I'm sure Captain Blood would be so proud."

Berry smirked knowingly. "I think not."

Laney chuckled in high spirits. *For once good news!* "Well, *I* approve, and I am part-Eleanor so..."

Berry grinned. "I've improved on certain aspects. It has a built-in interface so it can be configured independently of the quantum jump platform." He waved and the image of the map lattice behind him dissolved into the schematics of the Zeta device. "It has a compensator that renders the energy exchange negligible as long as it's under a certain threshold, similar to the anchor devices we'd used in the past to enable traveling to other dimensions."

"Cool," Laney murmured, looking over at Maia who was gazing up to study the specs on the screen herself.

Berry made another gesture and a hologram of a boomerang outline blinked in mid-air. "I've even programmed a 'boomerang' protocol on it, so you can keep track of your jumps and retrace your steps back to your original anchor point." He gave a slight shake of his head. "Of course, it's still not as fully-featured as Eleanor's original design, but I imagine it should do the trick." He held out the Zeta device as he finished.

Laney and Noah moved to take it at the same time. "How do I activate it?" they asked in unison.

Noah shot Laney a surprised look.

Laney met his gaze. "What?" she prompted flatly. "This is *my* mission," she said, turning to Berry before meeting Maia's carefully neutral yet wide-eyed look.

Berry fidgeted. "Um..."

"I'm sorry, *your* mission?" Noah's eyebrows were high on his forehead.

Laney's tone was stern. "Do you have a problem with that?"

"Uh—" Noah's thoughts were plain on his face.

"Hey," Berry interjected loudly before Noah could make his irate reply, knowing full well how easily their arguments tended to escalate. "Let's all just stay calm, shall we?"

Laney looked at Berry and Noah in turn. "Just because I'm the only one here whose brain isn't genetically super-advanced doesn't mean I can't handle things on my own," she reasoned, her tone carrying layers of perfectly justifiable pent-up frustration. "I never know where we are. I never know what's going on. And don't even get me started on everyone playing around with my brain like it's their own personal laboratory!"

Maia was grimacing, patting Laney's back to help settle her down.

But Laney went on with resolve. "I'm the one who doesn't belong here. I'm the only one who needs to go."

Berry wrinkled his nose, looking hesitant to argue with her.

But Noah gave her a mocking look. "Look," he started, his tone as calm as he could make it. "You don't know what you're going to run into in this other world."

Berry was already shaking his head. "I'm afraid I have to agree with Noah, Laney. I haven't even told you the tricky bit yet. We've still got quite a bit of work to do."

Maia looked over. "What does that mean?"

"Well," Berry started. "We know the target world. But there is literally an infinite number of paths you can take to get there. So we need to come up with the most expedient traversal path. One that goes through the least number of alternate worlds, not to mention the safest ones, in the shortest amount of time."

Laney looked tired already. "Traversal what?"

Berry waved his hand and the hologram of a polyhedron outline appeared above the table. "Understand that there are billions upon billions of multiverses. Our target world is this." He pointed to a dot near the edge of the shape and the image zoomed in to resolve back into the peanut lattice.

"We are...here." He pointed to another dot near the middle. "Interestingly," he interjected. "Your original world is *riiight* there," he said, pointing to about a few inches away from the second dot. "It's right around the maximum end of our quantum jump range."

"In any case, to get all the way over there—" He pointed to the edge dot again. "We're going to have to..." He moved his pointer finger to hop from one point to the other on the big map.

Laney's eyes popped out. "No way."

Noah was already shaking his head, his eyes closed in displeasure.

"Other dimensions indeed exist in the same space as us, but the way they're arranged, each quantum shear can only access within about every six times ten to the thirty-fourth's worlds away."

"Right."

Berry regarded Laney's short nod with a pause. "Um, okay," he tried to explain. "Let me try to simplify it—"

"No, no, I got it." Laney shook her head carelessly.

"You did?" Maia shot her an impressed look before exchanging looks with Berry. "She says she got it."

Laney rolled her eyes. "Come on, guys. I *can* learn."

"Either way," Berry continued with an almost apologetic smirk. "From this world, I'm afraid we can only execute a quantum jump to *one* other world, but not daisy-chain them together. We *have* been able to bounce probes through marginally further along to collect readings but not organic matter. And certainly not people."

"But it's possible?" Maia ventured, her eyebrows raised.

"I know Eleanor thought so," Berry relayed. "According to her notes. This approach is based on her theories. Her being sneaky and all, who knows?" He shrugged. "She might have already even tried jumping through to multiple worlds before and just never told anyone."

"How many worlds are we talking, Berry?" Noah asked.

"Just two," Berry reassured with a confident nod. Then he dropped his gaze to add in a mumble, "Or maybe three."

"You don't know for sure?" Noah looked exasperated.

"Heeey!" Berry put up his hands in defeat. "Like I said, this is all still theoretical."

"How do we even know which worlds we can go through?" Laney wanted to know.

Berry put up his finger. "Ah," he said, his eyes lighting up. "That I can tell you. Across the map, there are worlds similar enough to this world and yours that you can use them to hop across the multiverse. We've observed that in any of a hundred given worlds, there's a version of 'you' that quantum jumped to *this* world."

"Ohh."

"Yes, and you're going to have to piggyback your quantum

shear onto the exit traces of your jumps on those worlds to get to the next one."

She groaned. "I suppose I should just be glad I still understand what the hell you're saying."

"What's the target world like?" Noah queried.

"Okay, this is the tricky bit—"

"More tricky than what we're already talking about?" Laney put her hands up in disbelief.

"I'm afraid so," Berry said. "To access the supernova, we needed to find a space-faring world, a space-folding-capable society version of Earth."

"That seems simple enough."

"Except when you add that I've already plotted the exact supernova that we need," he added, making another gesture to change the hologram image back to display the constellation of Orion where Betelgeuse was located. "The only star big enough in the only alternate dimension we've found that will go nova in the right amount of time before our Laney—*you*—fades into oblivion, will go bye-bye...this week," he finished, already looking uncomfortable.

Laney was taken aback. "*This week*? You want me to do all that—jump and hop and piggyback—all this week?" She braced her hands on her head in panicked disbelief. "That's impossible!"

"So this might be a silly question given the timescales of galaxies, but can we wait for the next one?" Maia proposed.

Berry shrugged. "We can always wait, but who knows how long it will be before we find another one? It might not even be within our lifetime. Or worse, Eleanor never mentioned how long an 'exit trace' lasts for. By that time, they all might have degraded completely. She also didn't mention if you could reuse a specific exit trace twice, so we really have to be on-point here."

"This is impossible," Laney said again, her expression already devastated. Then she shook her head briskly as if to clear her head before she asked, "What are my other options?"

Berry looked regretful that he didn't have the right answer. "Well, you don't have any," he said. "You can't stay here because you can be sure The Alliance will be back to get you. Who knows what they're going to try to do next time?" he ventured, glancing at the others as if for support. "I mean the only other possibility is that you find a compatible parallel world with no Alliance. But so far, we haven't found one of those yet."

Laney gave him an expectant look. "You're saying even my world has Alliance? And I'm not talking the random rogue ones from your world like that guy who shot me eight months ago."

"Absolutely. The odds are you don't know they exist either or they're masquerading as some suspiciously creepy but legitimate form of government agency."

"Sounds like the CIA," she quipped.

"Or whomever. Which further supports my point," Berry continued as though he was defending a thesis on the matter. "There's no telling what kind of technology these agencies will have on these other worlds. You might run into ones that can detect a quantum shear jump in progress and can capture you as soon as you emerge. Some of them might even have technology that can disrupt the formation of a quantum shear altogether." He looked up at Noah. "Which is why your odds will be better having Noah there with you. He's specifically trained for these kinds of missions."

"Shucks, what a relief," Laney mumbled sarcastically.

Noah rolled his eyes but didn't say anything.

"It also goes without saying, you'd need to make sure that you do everything necessary to avoid your doubles seeing you in these other worlds. I can't stress enough how potentially catastrophic that would be. You don't want to contaminate the spacetime continuum any more than you already have."

Noah cleared his throat loudly, pointedly at the hint of blame in Berry's tone.

Laney had gone still, staring straight into thin air.

Berry put his hands up. "I'm not saying any of this is your fault," he resigned. "But you know? We need to be extra careful."

Laney didn't respond. She was frozen in her stance, her mouth slightly open.

"Laney?" Maia prompted, her forehead creasing in concern.

Then Laney's eyes widened in horror and she let out an ear-piercing shriek.

6

Primaries

Laney collapsed, still screaming, eyes open, her hands pressed tightly against either side of her head.

"What the hell is going on?" Noah's tone sounded almost panicked. He stood, alert in his stance, but looked unsure what he was supposed to do.

Maia rushed over to kneel by Laney's side to try to check on her even as she convulsed on the floor. "Her pulse is really fast. *Too* fast. And she's burning up."

Noah's HUD beeped at the same time that one of Berry's consoles let out a shrill sound, almost as shrill as Laney's screams.

"She's having a 'bleed through'," Noah noted loudly.

Maia shook her head. "This can't be a 'bleed through'. She's having a seizure!"

Berry cursed as he rushed toward the console, flicked open a little tab, and pressed a button. Whatever he'd triggered sent a sudden jolt right through Laney, but when she fell slack again, she stopped seizing on the floor, unconscious.

Berry blew out a breath.

"Was that—?" Noah began.

"Yeah."

Maia sank back on her heels then looked up at the two guys in turn. "Well, that can't be good."

Laney woke up coughing as she tried to sit up.

"Whoa." Berry supported her shoulder before she collapsed back down on the emergency stretcher.

She took a shivery breath, squinting as she looked around with only one eye open. She was still in the submarine but in a different, smaller compartment. She groaned after a moment. "Can I just say," she began, her voice croaky, "I'm so glad to be waking up *not* strapped to some type of chair or machine this time?"

Berry's grin was tentative.

"Was I out for long?"

He shook his head. "A half-hour maybe. Noah and Maia have started working on the traversal path on the map," he told her as she sat up slowly and regained her bearings.

She rubbed her hands over her arms for warmth. "So, was that what I think it was?"

"A bleed through?" He nodded. "Yes. My theory is that whatever else The Alliance tried to do to you, it's also corrupted your CCL."

Her hand flew up to the spot behind her ear where Berry

had attached the cerebral cortex link (CCL) for monitoring her 'bleed throughs' a few days ago.

Laney let out a heavy sigh, closing her eyes for a moment. "Are you kidding me?" She couldn't even begin to describe how relieved she had been that she hadn't had a single incident of an alternate version of her overtaking her consciousness in over a day. She was almost hopeful that in that respect, she'd been cured. And now this. "I thought the 'bleed throughs' had gone."

Berry cringed, hesitant to explain. "Not quite. They may have just gone into a type of remission, probably caused by some lingering side effects of being in that horror show Alliance machine. But it seems to be dissipating."

"So, that means they're going to come back," Laney deduced.

"And probably worse. I'm so sorry. I had to zap you to stop it. Otherwise, the 'bleed through' might have liquefied your brain."

Laney blinked hard. "Jeez, don't worry about candy-coating it for me then."

Berry winced. "Sorry. Again." He gritted his teeth, looking sheepish. "I'm thinking we have to extract your CCL altogether, in case there are any other adverse side effects."

Laney shivered again.

Berry assessed her with another look. "Are you sure you're okay?"

She waved her hand. "Fine," she dismissed. "Just a bit chilly."

"Oh." Berry's eyes lit up and he walked across the room. "Not for nothing, but I nearly had to strong-arm Noah into going to get started on the work instead of sitting here waiting for you to wake up. Well," he paused to correct. "Not me. Maia." He came back to hand her a weighted blanket. "He was really worried about you," he told her, a catch in his tone.

"Really?" She drew her eyebrows together in skepticism, throwing the blanket around her shoulders. "I thought he for one would be relieved if my brain liquefied. Then none of you all would have to go through all this pokey, scary-ass, dangerous work.

Berry nudged her shoulder lightly. "That's not true. You're one of us now. We care about you. And if Noah wasn't such a stiff, I'm sure he'd tell you the same thing."

She grinned, even as she simply shook her head in disbelief, as she examined a few things on the instrument table, a soldering iron catching her eye, and she frowned slightly as a fragment of memory popped up in her head.

"Hey Berry," Laney called out, hesitantly. "The last time I was here, you said something about—why did you—how did you...know?" She wrinkled her nose. "That Noah and I...uh..."

"Oh." Berry raised his eyebrows. "How could I have been so incredibly perceptive as to infer that you guys had already made out that first day as though I had a spy camera watching you guys the whole time?"

Laney's face turned red.

He bit back his smirk but went on to explain. "There's a theory, see," he began. "*The Primaries Theory*. Eleanor postulated it herself," he relayed offhand.

"It asserts that, across each of all the parallel worlds, there's only one genuine copy of each of us. It's not guaranteed to be the best version of us *per se*, but the theory is that *that* version was the mold, where each of us began. Our primary."

Laney nodded, surprisingly able to follow his explanation so far.

He regarded her with a look. "Do you believe in soul-mates?"

She was unsure what that had to do with anything, but she shrugged anyway. "I don't know. I'm not sure. I guess I thought I did."

Berry looked amused. "Well, there's an auxiliary principle to The Primaries Theory. That when the primary version of ourselves finds the primary version of our soulmate—that's it. Fireworks, explosions, you name it."

He paused meaningfully. "And I think, like it or not, that's why you and Noah..." He cleared his throat instead of finishing his sentence.

Laney blushed furiously in utter shock. "What?"

"Some people are lucky enough to spawn in the same 'verse as their primary mate, but some just don't, so they wander around their world and settle for the closest thing. They aren't really soulmates, and they themselves can tell, but they don't have any choice."

Laney's mind was reeling as she recalled Eleanor's words, the way she had spoken about Noah.

I know he loves me so much and all that, but I'll tell you some-thing, I always kind of knew maybe I wasn't built for that kind of stuff...

"Of course, that's only a theory," Berry recanted, studying her expression. "But I reckon it's a damn good one."

Laney's jaw felt unhinged from how low the new revelation

had made her drop it. Then another thought occurred to her. "And Noah knows this," she breathed in realization.

"Yup."

"And Maia. You've *all* known about this all along?" Laney asked again, still in bewildered disbelief as pieces of random previous conversations somehow all finally fully formed the puzzle. They had all known it. She smacked her forehead with her palm in realization. "Oh jeez, Eleanor! *That's* how she also knew that Noah and I had kissed."

Berry was still smirking.

Laney gawked at him. "It's not funny."

"Are you sure?"

She narrowed her eyes and Berry put up his hands as if in defeat wordlessly.

No wonder every other guy Laney had encountered in this world so far was giving her a wide berth. They knew who she was. And they all knew she already had a primary. Someone whom they figure could probably give them a decent enough thumping with a mere look if they even breathed wrong.

But it was still just a theory, right? It could still be a hundred percent wrong. That didn't mean it explained why Laney had always felt she had such a strong connection to Noah. It could all just be a coincidence.

More to the point, it didn't mean she had to do anything about it. In fact, it was worse now. Who's to say that this grand theory wasn't making any of them see or feel things that weren't actually there? There was no way to know for sure. It was only yet another way that she was being manipulated.

Stupid theory. *It changes nothing.*

"Hey, you're up." Maia's smile looked relieved as she entered the room and walked up to where Laney was sitting.

"Mm-hm," Laney murmured, her lips still curled in displeasure.

Maia looked over at Berry. "What's going on?"

Berry didn't respond. He just shrugged and took a backward step, headed out of the room and away from the two of them.

Maia met Laney's gaze again. "Did I miss something?"

"And just exactly when were you planning to tell me?" Laney tilted her head to one side. "You know for someone who can't keep a secret, you certainly kept the lid shut tight on this one."

"You lost me. The lid on what?" Maia blinked.

She narrowed her eyes again. "Your lab assistant. And Simon," she listed. "You knew what all those guys were running scared from. Or more accurately *who*."

Maia's mouth formed an 'o' as it clicked what Laney was referring to. "Ohhh. You mean why nobody wants to get close to you because everyone knows you're Noah's primary?" She clenched her teeth sheepishly. "Yeah...sorry, but it's kind of like you're spoken for."

"But I wasn't even his girlfriend!" Laney insisted. "It was the other Laney. Oh, this is *so* not fair!" She folded her arms across her chest, annoyed.

"What's the matter?" Maia asked expectantly. "I thought you would be relieved. Now you understand, Eleanor was never the one for him. You two can be together." She elbowed her lightly in encouragement.

"That's not what that means. And that's not even the

point!" She rolled her eyes, annoyed, trying to refocus on her argument. "I already have a boyfriend. I can't just—just—"

Maia was looking at her in a way that said she wasn't buying it.

Laney blew out a breath, exasperated. "Just when I thought this world could not get any weirder," she commented.

"Oh, come on." Maia slung her arm around Laney's shoulders. "We're growing on you a little bit, aren't we?"

That made Laney chuckle, her mood lightening as she regarded Maia's comical expression. "What about you? I just realized it hadn't occurred to me to ask." She looked curious. "Do you have a...husband, boyfriend, fiancé?"

"Are you kidding me?" Maia gave her a funny look as she straightened up. "I'm married to my work. Most of us are." She gestured around to nothing in particular. "Can you imagine it? With all these scientists, with something like the Primaries theory being kicked around? We're all too cerebral to risk it. That is simply a place only the brave dare go."

She shrugged in faraway thought. "Of course, some people still do the whole marriage and kids bit. But later, you know, after pursuing their career goals, reaching their aspirations. Maybe I will someday too, but right now, it's more important to discover the genetic secrets of the multiverse," she concluded, wiggling her eyebrows.

Laney nodded in understanding.

Maia gave her a sideways glance. "Besides, there's only one reason anyone would ever propose a commitment like that."

"What?"

She gave her a meaningful look. "Because they're really

sure," she stated, a tinge of commendation in her tone. "That Noah's a rare breed."

Laney resisted the urge to roll her eyes again. "I'm sure he is." She had no doubt he was a rare breed. But of what? *That* she wasn't sure.

Maia jerked her thumb in the direction of the main chamber. "If you're feeling better, you should go check out that map. Berry's 'brane' thing is absolutely amazing and some of these other dimensions are mind-blowing!"

"Of course *you* would think so," Laney quipped with a grin.

"Interestingly, one dimension is a musical. Everyone sings everything. Can you imagine it? I would totally rock that world!"

Laney made a face. "Jeez, please don't tell me we need to go to that one."

Maia laughed. "Nope! Noah, of course, nipped that plan right in the bud. By the way, you're gonna wanna get in on that. You know, given that you—never know where you're going, or what's going on, or everyone's using your brain as...what was it? A personal playground?" she finished, her expression slightly mocking.

"Thanks for the support." Laney shook her head in feigned derision. "You're supposed to be my best friend."

Maia looked surprised. "I'm your best friend?"

Laney stopped short, momentarily caught off-guard. "Um, sure," she replied with a shrug. "In this world, why not?"

Maia's smile was wide. She nudged Laney's shoulder. "Anyway," she started. "What I came here to tell you. I got a message from the University and I have to pop out for a bit. Besides, it's almost midnight and I need my beauty sleep."

She smiled back. "Sure. You coming back to see me off in the morning?"

"Definitely."

"Well, gotta go. World-class laboratories don't run themselves, you know?"

Laney chuckled, mimicking a little salute. "*Ciao.*"

"Hey!" Maia gave her two thumbs up in approval as she walked away.

7

Timetable

Laney craned her neck as she passed a huffy Noah on his way out through the doorway as she was walking back to Berry's holographic map table. She raised her eyebrows, not stopping. "Noah's upset," she stated. "Must be Thursday."

Berry chuckled. "Don't mind him. He's having some kind of existential dilemma." He pulled down the strange contraption over his eyes which looked like brass magnifying goggles and turned his attention back to the instrument table beside him. One of his little robot pals was holding steady a small silver cylinder, while Berry fiddled with a vaguely familiar-looking gadget that caught Laney's eye.

"What is that?"

"It's Maia's memory serum again. Obviously, we can't return you to your homeworld remembering all of this," he relayed. "Once you're clear of Eleanor's tracking solution,

Noah will drop you off at your world, give you another hit of this before he comes back here."

She bit her lip warily. "Is that a good idea?" she asked. "We had enough trouble undoing it the last time around."

"Well, all going well, there won't be any need to undo this next round. I mean, you'll have missed about a week from your world that you won't be able to explain but trust me, it's better than being burdened with all this knowledge."

Laney watched as Berry carefully filled the small gadget with the serum, her thoughts turning to the last eight months of not remembering what she had gone through in this world the first time.

It seemed absurd that she would just go on to live her life as though none of this will have happened. However, she couldn't argue with his point. It would be too difficult to go back to her old life otherwise. And there were definitely certain events that she wouldn't want to remember.

And certain people...

She shook it off with a small sigh, studying the big holographic map to try to distract herself with actually important things. "How's the traversal path coming along?"

"Oh, we're still running the search, taking certain factors into consideration, you know, the world has to have a nitrogen-rich atmosphere, where English is still an understood language, humans haven't evolved into quadrupeds, that sort of thing," he listed, almost absently.

Laney couldn't help an amused shake of her head.

Berry reached wide to click a few buttons on a different console and the holographic screen overlay a red progress bar onto the map. "Looks like it's at...thirty percent. It should be done in the morning."

Laney gazed up at the map forlornly. "Are you sure we're going to be able to do this? It's such a *big* map. I mean where do we even start looking?"

For a change, Berry gave her a reassuring smile, even with half his face covered with his magnifying goggles. "Well, the good news is, in about a few dozen worlds at least, Eleanor and I will have already marked where the portals are between dimensions," he told her. "I mean I can't guarantee that all the markers will still be in their original locations, but then you can use the Zeta device to detect them."

"What did you use as markers?"

"Oh, just something inconspicuous," he drawled, focused on his work. "Something we'd found almost always existed in any world."

"What was it?"

"You've seen them already. We had a bunch of them back at my office at GNR," he reminded her. "Traffic cones."

"What?" Laney's expression was of skeptical disbelief.

Berry thought he needed to explain. "You know, one of those reflective orange cones you always see at construction sites."

Laney dismissed him. "No, I know what they are," she said. "Are you telling me that there are orange cones in my world that are actually markers for portals between worlds?"

"Precisely."

Laney let out a short laugh. She gazed up to watch traversal paths displayed at random across the map as the search algorithm worked. *Fascinating...*

She shook her head again. "You know I was never a girl scout, but I always did like maps. I mean my family never traveled much." She sounded wistful. "But looking at maps always made me think that there's such a big world out there, I would never run out of places to explore if I had the chance. Like, the possibilities were just infinite," she said, her eyes gleaming.

Berry grinned, looking up. "Maybe there's a little bit of scientist in you after all."

She chuckled. "Mind you, I'd probably still get lost all the time," she amended. "It's too bad that locator device thingy is gone now, huh? I should have kept it instead of giving it back to Eleanor."

"What locator device?" Berry prompted offhand, pulling up the goggles off his face as he moved to get another gadget that the little robot was handing up to him.

"Oh. I mean, that necklace, you know the one I'm talking about," Laney replied with a prompting wave.

But Berry looked like he couldn't breathe. "What?"

"Back in Paris, eight months ago," she said, matter-of-factly. "You know, Noah gave me that necklace that used to be Eleanor's? The one with the cool antique clock thing on it? The lo-jack device."

"The lo-jack device," he echoed, his voice lowering. "You gave it to Eleanor?"

"Yeah, why?" Laney narrowed her eyes at the funny expression on Berry's face.

"You...gave Eleanor...the transdimensional locator beacon."

"Yes. Why?" Laney repeated, still at a loss.

Berry's jaw had dropped slightly. "The beacon system is still online, back at my office at GNR."

"Sssooo...?"

He coughed. "It means we might have a way to locate Laney! The real Laney."

"What? Really? That's great!"

Berry instantly stopped short, his expression neutralizing. "Don't tell Noah."

For the first time ever, it sounded like Berry was giving *her* orders. She looked taken aback. "What? Why not?"

He screwed up his face. "Look, it's just—he can get really obsessed," he explained. "It's-it's not healthy. He'll just be distracted from this mission. And our priority is to deliver you home safe and sound. That's all." His eyes were urgent. "Just please, promise, you won't tell him."

She blinked. "You're asking me to keep this from him? This is a pretty big deal," she pointed out. "So, what, he'll never find out where the real Laney went?"

Berry waved it away. "*I'll* tell him. Look, I promise I will, but not until after we've sorted you out first. Alright? Do we have a deal?" His eyebrows were raised expectantly.

"Sure, okay."

"Laney, I'm being totally serious right now. You *cannot* tell him," he pressed.

"Fine, fine. Mum's the word," Laney assured, gesturing zipping up her lips.

Then Berry dropped his gaze and put two fingers against his ear. "Yeah."

Laney knit her eyebrows. "What?"

Berry held up a finger to signal quiet before speaking

again. "It's all set up?" Then he nodded. "Good." He dropped his hand and looked up at Laney again.

"What was that?"

Berry gestured to his ear. "I embedded my walkie-talkie in my inner ear." He patted his little robot before slipping the memory serum gadget inside a little black pouch and beckoning Laney over. "Come on. I have something else to show you."

"Why, Dr. Berry Vermillion, you built a quantum jump platform on the submarine?"

Laney easily recognized the highly imposing glass-and-mirrors platform similar to the one she had arrived onto this world five days ago.

An ethereal green light was already shining up from underneath the platform, indicating that it was already activated. Another handful of people wearing white lab coats and safety goggles were purposefully adjusting dials and turning knobs on several control panels arranged in racks to calibrate the machine.

"Moved, actually," Berry corrected. "This is the same one from GNR. The smaller version. I managed to adapt the sub's power source to boost the reactor. Mind you, it wasn't easy. I almost thought I wouldn't be able to get it to work in time."

Laney grinned at him. "You know what? I think you underestimate yourself," she said, patting Berry's back. "You're the smartest person I know. Why else do you think Eleanor kept you around?"

"How about 'easy to boss around'?" Berry supplied with an

ironic smirk as they walked toward one of the control panels around the platform. "I should put it on my resume."

Laney laughed.

Just then, a set of doors to a closet in the corner, what must have been the armory, swung open with a thud, and Laney and Berry both turned to look in time to see Noah come out.

He was holding two big laser rifles, a belt of pressure grenades slung over his shoulder, two handguns peeking from his back pockets, and several other more subtle-looking weapons on a utility belt around his waist.

Berry shook his head quickly. "Oh. You can't bring those weapons."

Noah looked at Berry like he was crazy. "Can't bring weapons? Are you kidding?"

"It's already enough of a risk bringing any of our technology through to other worlds," Berry rationalized. "It would be too dangerous to bring any more. Like I said we want to make sure what we do has the smallest impact on the spacetime continuum. Otherwise, we might run into some more...problems," he finished, sounding hesitant.

Laney watched his face carefully. "Why do I get the feeling that you're not telling us absolutely everything?"

"Because if I told you absolutely everything, you'd likely flip out and run out that door screaming." Berry gave each of them a look to advise, "You need to blend in. Be incognito."

Noah glowered in displeasure but he began to unload himself of the weapons, plunking them one by one onto a table.

Laney was wearing the usual clothes she wore to school, jeans, and a monogrammed sweater, what she was wearing when she arrived in their world. She looked over at Noah, gesturing to his attire with a critical look. "Are you going like that?"

Noah glanced down at himself before meeting her gaze, the slightest look of offense in his eyes. "What?"

"Well," she began pointedly. "That jacket makes you look like you're about to join an airstrike over Germany. In 1939."

He tugged on the bottom of his vintage flight jacket obstinately. "I love this jacket."

"I think what Laney means is—" Berry cut off as Noah's dark glare turned toward him and he put up his hands in surrender, finishing loudly with, "Is we all love the jacket, don't we? Looks great."

Laney noticed some of the lab coats nearby who'd overheard were exchanging mirthful looks and she chuckled.

Noah narrowed his eyes at her but she gave him an undaunted look.

"That reminds me," he started, walking up to her.

"What?"

"We'll need to work out some sort of signal," Noah proposed, his tone all business.

"For what?"

"We don't know exactly what we're going to find out there," he reminded her, glancing over at Berry who was preoccupied with configuring the control panel. "It's going to be dangerous."

"Why are you saying that like I don't know it's going to be dangerous? Of course I know it'll be dangerous. What about any of this is even remotely safe?" she asked, making a face.

He cleared his throat. "I'm just saying, maybe we need a

code word. Something to signal trouble. Something that stays between us." His voice lowered on his last statement and Laney caught a hint of intensity in his eyes. But it was gone as fast as it came.

She swallowed. "Okay."

He tilted his head and she realized he was waiting for her to suggest something.

"Oh." She shot him a look. "I'm sorry. Are you under the impression that I come up with code words in my every-day life?"

"No." He looked at her. "I'm giving you the prerogative to come up with one. It's called manners."

She made a show of shrugging. "I don't know. How do you come up with a code word anyway?"

"It needs to be a neutral word. Or a phrase. Something innocuous. Something that can flag if something is wrong."

"How about 'Help me. Something is wrong.'?"

He frowned at her cavalier attitude. "Are you going to take this seriously or not?"

Laney's shoulders shook in mirth. "Alright, fine, Mr. Bond. What do *you* usually use in your super-secret spy missions?"

Noah pursed his lips at her sarcastic tone. "What's your favorite food?"

She stopped to think. "Are we talking cuisine or all-time favorite? Or dessert? Because you know that's a completely different category altogether—"

"For crying out loud." He groaned in exasperation. "What about least favorite food? I already know you hate tomatoes."

"You want the code word to be 'tomatoes'?" She looked skeptical.

"Fine! So not food then?"

"Like what?"

"I don't know." He looked around, trying to think. "Maybe something to do with science?"

"You think a science word will be innocuous?" She resisted the urge to laugh.

"How about 'relativity'?"

"What? I can't say that. That's ridiculous."

"It's better than tomatoes," Noah pointed out.

"Better *how*?" She gave him a stubborn, expectant look.

He rolled his eyes. "Alright then! *Not* 'relativity'. But we have to decide on something."

Laney rubbed her forehead. "Jeez, I feel like I'm taking a pop quiz right now. Are you sure we need to have a code word?"

Noah groaned out loud again, looking like he wanted to start tearing his hair out in frustration. "Laney—!"

There was a loud explosion from outside.

Noah's eyes lit up in alert.

"What was that?" Berry asked, reaching over to flick some buttons on some panels to show the surveillance outside the submarine.

The night having fallen was making the view hard to see, but it looked like something was burning right by the terminal building, and black smoke obviously *not* coming from the cross-country train was wafting downwind.

Just then there was another explosion.

"Is that outside? What's going on?" Laney leaned over Berry's shoulder to see.

Berry put his fingers to his ear again, listening on his internal walkie-talkie. "Terrorists...?"

Noah huffed. "The Alliance."

Laney's eyes widened. "What? The Alliance is back? Already?" She balked in skepticism. "Don't these people have day jobs?"

"It's the middle of the night," Noah reminded her.

"Still," she mocked obstinately.

"Oh boy." Berry almost leaped across to several other control panels, pushing buttons frantically. "All hands, we're casting off," he said loudly on the PA. "We have to go. Now! Now!" He hit another button and something made a loud whooshing sound at the same time that the sub pushed off from the dock.

Laney swayed on her feet and she held on to one side of a control panel as the sub jerked sideways. Noah was looking around, on his guard, and he cast a glance at the table full of weapons.

"Jeez, that was close!" Berry remarked, continuously fiddling with the control boards, before checking the surveillance again. "Uh guys, I think our timetable has just been pushed up."

"What?" Laney nearly squeaked. "We're not ready, are we?"

Berry's back was to her so she couldn't see what he was doing, but after a moment, he turned around. "Give me your hand," he instructed.

And even before Laney could question further or move, he leaned over and deftly attached something to her wrist.

"Here," he said. "You hang on to Zeta device." He met her

gaze evenly. "Let's say for the record: it is *your* mission," he declared with a smile.

Laney gave him an appreciative look. "Thanks," she said, giving the Zeta device a cursory appraising scan. It was strapped to her wrist on a brace with an ornate latch.

He put his hand on her shoulder to relay, "Now you don't want to get stuck in some random alternate dimension, so you have to make sure you and Noah stay together."

"Oh, fabulous."

The next explosion must have been in the water as the impact was enough to make the entire submarine shudder.

"Berry," Noah called out his warning, his eyes focused on what was outside the big windows in front of the sub.

"Holy cats." Berry shooed Laney toward the jump platform. "I bet they'll be gunning for my power reactor and let me tell you, it's not exactly industry-standard. You two better go before they break out their anti-submarine weapons."

"No, wait!" Laney threw up her hands. "We don't even have the complete traversal path yet." She glanced back and forth from Berry to Noah.

"There's no time. We'll have to do it on the fly," Noah replied, running around to grab certain things in preparation.

"Do it on the fly—well, that sounds like a genius plan. I wonder what can go wrong with that?"

Berry was hurriedly clicking buttons and flicking switches to configure the jump platform. "We can use your homeworld as a launch point. That should be safe enough."

"Time to go!" Noah hollered, walking past Laney.

Her eyes lit up as she remembered something else. "Hey, my CCL—!" she called out to Berry. She still had it on.

"I'm sorry, Laney. We don't have time," Berry yelled, slamming on a big red button on the console behind him.

The wind rose as the quantum shear ignited upon the jump platform.

Noah stepped up to it and turned back to look at Laney.

Laney was staring at the swirling vortex of doom, already breathing heavily in panic, anticipation, anxiety.

"Are you ready?"

"Are you kidding?"

"Here goes nothing."

"Good luck."

8

Homeworld

Laney took a step forward and did a 360-degree survey of her surroundings.

Only the faint sounds of crickets filtered through the trees that lined the deserted paved walkway leading up to the dorms and back toward the school clinic. It was dark but the gardens at the quad were still the same shade of green that she remembered.

Laney took a deep breath.

She was back.

She was home.

It was pretty bizarre to think that she had successfully traveled back to her dimension again. It wasn't even the first time. She hadn't acknowledged yet how normal it was starting to feel for her to be jumping through quantum shears either, to be journeying through parallel worlds.

It was a little bit exhilarating, sure. But freaky.

She turned to look at the space where the quantum shear had dissolved into nothing.

There was no telling if The Alliance had caught up to the sub or if the sub had already been sunk or destroyed. There was also no telling if the explosions in the dock were isolated there or if they had reached further into town.

She frowned. All she could do was hope that Maia and Berry were okay.

Then she heard Noah coughing. His head was bent low, his hands propped on his knees. He seemed to be having difficulty breathing.

Laney almost forgot that quantum jumps were supposed to have that effect because you've basically been squeezed through a singularity and stretched at an atomic level.

But the odds were that because of the interdimensional insulation that Eleanor had dosed her with, quantum jumps didn't affect Laney that way, which, unfortunately, was the only fortunate thing about it.

She watched Noah warily. She wanted to go over to help him but she was still feeling on edge about having been rushed to start their impossible, highly theoretical mission.

Not to mention, she was feeling quite skittish about Berry's revelation regarding "primaries." The situation was complicated enough. And counter to all her efforts of trying to stay away from him for the past day or so, there they were, just the two of them. Again.

When Noah finally straightened up, he met her somber gaze. Then he dropped his eyes back down to his HUD, prob-ably to check that they were in the right place.

Laney narrowed her eyes upon seeing the HUD flicker

above his arm. It was the first time she'd seen it again up close since her recovery from the hospital.

Noah had never really explained where he had gotten it from. And as far as she had seen, only one other person in his world had anything like it.

The Alliance agent named Jacob.

Only Alliance carry this tech...

There was a sinking feeling in Laney's stomach as she glared at the HUD like it would self-destruct if she stared long enough, but when Noah looked over again, she averted her gaze.

His eyebrows furrowed a little as he noticed, but he didn't comment on it. "So we're back," he concluded, looking around before gesturing to the Zeta device. "Are you getting anything?"

Laney remembered that this time around, for a change, she also had a gadget. She checked the little device on her wrist, flicking the holographic screen on, but there were so many numbers and symbols swimming about on it.

She frowned again, trying to focus. The Zeta device might be a revolutionary little thing but it wasn't very intuitive. Leave it to Berry to design something probably only he could decipher.

Noah registered her lost expression. "Give it to me."

It was the combination of anxiety and trepidation, layered with newfound suspicion, that Laney clutched at her arm, shooting him a sharp look.

He gave her a look of disbelief. "I just want to synchronize it with my HUD," he told her. "What's gotten into you?"

"Nothing!" Her tone a clear indication of the opposite.

"Are you still on about this being 'your' mission?" He gestured air quotes sarcastically.

She didn't reply.

Noah looked at her steadily. "Look, I'm not very good with people, but I can tell when someone's avoiding me. And it doesn't take a genius to know that something's bothering you. Now, what is it?"

Laney pursed her lips.

Noah was a traitor and he'd been rightly accused of double-crossing, even triple-crossing, other people before.

She was torn between reason and something undefined, something that wouldn't stop nagging her. Perhaps the urge to know, to have him defend himself, to have him prove none of it was true. That he was anything other than what one might easily conclude he was: a bad guy.

"Laney, I need to know in case it affects our mission," he stated. He studied her expression before he asked, "What did Jacob tell you?"

Her eyes widened slightly at his perceptiveness.

"Did he tell you I worked for The Alliance?"

Laney met his gaze, looking even more bewildered. "Yes," she replied after a moment.

Noah tilted his head, giving her an incredulous mocking look.

"What? I mean, you have a HUD," she rationalized hoarsely, trying to make her point while not risking being too loud. "It's Alliance tech! And you couldn't show it around The Community because The Alliance is a super-secret organization." She dropped her gaze at the jumble of thoughts in her head. "And you're really good at keeping secrets. And betraying people.

Who knows what kinds of tricks you've got up those vintage sleeves and who you're going to throw under the bus the next time around?" she finished, giving him an accusing look.

His response was steady. "No, you're right."

She blinked. She didn't think he would just flat out admit it. "Huh?"

"Laney," he began, sounding calm. "I had a HUD installed, because last year, I did join The Alliance," he relayed and went on to add before her worst fears could be confirmed. "But undercover."

Her eyes lit up.

"To help locate Eleanor."

Laney's jaw dropped slightly as the revelation dawned in her eyes.

Noah shrugged. "And Jacob found out. That's why they obviously aren't very happy with me because they think I stole their tech." He held his arm closer to her so she could inspect it. "But as you can see, it's integrated to me now. It's not like I can just return it."

Laney furrowed her eyebrows. "No?"

He shook his head.

It hit her again. What Noah was willing to go through for Eleanor, the sacrifices he was willing to make. Who knew what he'd had to go through to join The Alliance? What kind of process was required to integrate technology into humans like that? It couldn't have just been a pinprick. But he did it.

He did it all. As always.

For Eleanor.

His eyes softened. "So do you trust me now?"

She gave him a wary look. "You still keep an awful lot of secrets."

He met her gaze, his eyebrows raised. "Don't *you* have secrets?"

Laney stiffened as she remembered a particular whopper of a one, one she'd been specifically instructed to keep from him.

But he didn't press and just bit back a smirk. "Now, can I have a look at the Zeta device?" He held his hand out. "Please."

She sighed and obliged, holding up her wrist so Noah could configure the Zeta device to synchronize with his HUD, even as she watched him carefully.

Maybe he explained the HUD but that didn't mean she needed to trust him. At the end of the day, she had to remember this was really *her* mission. And hers alone.

She gave herself a mental shake to attempt to settle her unease.

"Look." His tone was gentle as he leaned his head slightly toward hers to point something out on the gadget. "There's the anchor for the 'boomerang' protocol." He swiped across the display. "If you nudge this, it shows you where we came from, and here's where we are right now. These are the coordinates of your homeworld."

She nodded as she took note, shivering again, despite her long-sleeved sweater. It was an easy reminder that she was back in the northern hemisphere with its brisk climate.

Noah gave her a once-over. "Are you okay?" he asked a little more than curiously as he finished up with the Zeta device and let go of her wrist.

"Just a little cold."

He sniffed. "Now you're wishing you had a jacket like mine."

And despite all her reservations, that unexpected quip *from Noah* made her stifle a sudden, snorted laugh such that she had to look around vigilantly to make sure nobody had heard.

She gave him a wry, bemused look. "Honestly," she spoke after a pause. "You look like you should be at some type of postmodern renaissance fair or something." "That should have tipped me off right from the start. I should have known when we first met that there was no way you were the real Jake Donovan."

"But you didn't."

"Please, I was all panicked. You were acting like a total psycho," she recalled, rolling her eyes. "You couldn't just talk to me like a real person?"

"Remember I tried that too the next time around? You still thought I was crazy," Noah reminded her before referring back to his HUD as they proceeded down the walkway.

"Could you blame me? In case you forgot, here in *my* world, we don't live our daily lives concerned with the fate of multiple universes. I honestly don't envy you people who have to live with these types of concerns," she drawled, looking around the gardens again.

All going well, she *would* be back home in a week and forget about everything. Only, the damage will have already been done. To Noah's world. To Eleanor.

She wasn't sure she wanted to live with that, even if she wouldn't be able to remember.

"Do you think after all this," Laney mused, looking gloomy.

"Berry could just send me back to that first day? Like last time? That way all this would never have happened."

He shook his head. "I'm not sure the small-scale jump platform can manage that. It won't have enough grunt."

"Oh."

"In any case," Noah went on. "It's probably not a good idea. It's been too long. Too much will have already changed. And like Berry said, we don't want to affect spacetime any more than we have to." He gave her a meaningful shrug. "We need to accept that some things are...inevitable."

9

The Odds

Laney felt off-balance for a second, almost tripping over her own feet, and Noah caught her arm. "Oh, sorry," she said, straightening up. "I guess going through the shear this time's actually got to me a little bit."

But Noah's forehead was creased. He took a quick look around. "No. I felt that too. What the hell *was* that?" He checked his HUD again. "Something just happened to this world."

Laney was craning her neck to look at his HUD herself. "What do you mean?"

"I'm not sure." Noah took a deep breath, betraying a little apprehension on his face. "We'd better locate that exit trace before we're too late." He gestured to the Zeta device.

But Laney didn't have to check her wrist. "I still remember. It's this way," she said as she moved past him toward the thicket along the walkway.

And true enough, after a few more yards, Noah spoke up to note, "There's the traffic cone."

Laney looked over toward where Noah was pointing and she spotted a slightly bent orange traffic cone by the gutter. As they approached it, she could see it looked like it had seen better days but at least it was still there.

"So," she began, twirling around on her heels. "Of all the spots in all the membranes in all the multiverses, this is where it is. Right past the gym at my boring old high school."

Noah hunched down beside the orange cone.

Laney watched with vague interest. "You're just going to open the quantum shear back up? How does that work anyway?"

Noah replied even as he was concentrating on his HUD. "Well, if you recall your M-theory physics," he began with an obvious satirical tone. "All the dimensions in the multiverse are separated by thin membranes. Like a curtain. And if you give these curtains a good enough shake—"

"Ah. Then you can pass through them," she finished with a nod, ignoring his little veiled insult. She shook her head. "Well, I still can't believe it. And all this time," she mused. "This dirty old thing has been spying on my world and nobody ever noticed. Nobody even cared. You see these things lying about in the strangest places, honestly. I've seen a picture of one someone had put on top of this like seventy-foot-tall pine tree." She paused in thought. "Huh. They said it was a prank, but now I have to wonder, maybe it was actually a portal marker."

Noah stopped short, his eyes narrowing slightly and he put a finger to his lips. "Sshh."

Laney ducked slightly as she looked around. But the sound that she heard made her face brighten. "Oh my gosh, that's Darla!"

The mere sound of her friend's voice lifted her mood instantly. She eagerly moved toward the sound, peering through a gap in the thicket to try to see. She figured Darla and Kevin were hanging out at one of the benches behind the dorms.

"I can hear her. And Kevin too." Then she smirked. "Those two. It's totally after hours. They shouldn't be out this late. We got into so much trouble the last time we all did this," she relayed with a small chuckle. "I'm totally going to tell the R.A. the next time I see her. Oh—" Laney shot Noah a pleading look. "Could I say hi to them? Just for a second? Pretty please? I mean, it's been five days. They must be worried sick by now, not to mention my parents."

"Laney," Noah began, his expression carefully blank. "I don't think you should make a sudden appearance and raise their hopes unnecessarily. At least, not yet," he added.

"Not yet," she echoed in displeasure. "You're such a party pooper. I mean, look, they're right there." She moved a few branches away for Noah to be able to see as she gestured toward her two friends. "It would literally only take—" She stopped short from her sneer of ridicule. "Wait, what? Why is he holding her hand?" She frowned, confused.

The next moment, Kevin leaned over to kiss Darla.

Full. Right on the mouth.

Laney's jaw dropped in shock. *What the damn hell?*

"Good night, babe," Kevin whispered with a wave and a smile, to which Darla replied with a smile of her own before they both stood up and walked off in different directions.

Laney felt her stomach somersault. She felt sick, frozen, paralyzed. What the hell was going on? Was it even possible? Were they cheating on her?

She'd only been gone for five days.

But what if that was enough time for them to develop a relationship? Maybe their feelings had grown over the loss they both felt from Laney having disappeared.

Laney shook her head briskly, unable to process what she'd just seen. It couldn't be real.

She felt something shift again, as though something invisible passing right through her, and she held on to Noah's arm, but she was too upset to think about anything else right then.

"It happened again. You felt that, right?" Noah asked her, checking on his HUD again at the same time furtively looking around.

"Felt what? The knife in my back from my backstabbing friends?" Laney wanted to throw up. There was a lump in her throat and she felt like she was about to cry.

Noah was frowning over his HUD readings. "We should go now."

She was still shaking her head, more than willing to let disbelief overtake devastation for the moment. "I don't understand. This doesn't make any sense."

"Focus, Laney!" Noah snapped, bracing his hands on her shoulders. He gave her a steady look. "I have a theory," he supplied. "But we have to find the quantum shear trace first if you wanted to be able to return here permanently."

Laney blinked up at him, his words coming through to her.

She needed to fix herself and get rooted back to her own

world. Only then could she deal with whatever the hell was going on with Kevin and Darla.

She started to nod. First things first. "Right. You're right. Let's do it."

Noah returned the nod before he began to work on his HUD to manipulate the quantum shear into reforming right by where the orange cone indicated.

And just like before, just like it always did, a tear in the current reality appeared in the form of the gaping mouth of a black hole.

Laney looked around, her hair whipping in her face in the sudden gusty wind, with everything around them turning reddish in hue as the quantum shear sucked in every other color of the light spectrum.

"Okay. That seemed to work. It's reading the coordinates of the next world."

She tilted her head. "I thought the traversal path never completed. What are you, guessing right now?" she prompted in skepticism.

"These dimensional coordinates were on the list of safe worlds cataloged from the project last year," he informed her. "It should be fine."

She wasn't exactly buying it. "Well, it *looks* like your garden variety swirling vortex of doom alright. How do we know it's going to the right place?"

Noah gave her a deadpan look. "What, you want me to redial? It's not an international phone call, Laney."

"Maybe we need to test it first. What if something's wrong and we vaporize the moment we go through there?"

"Exactly how do you propose we test it?"

"I don't know. Throw something in there. Stick your hand in."

"What about *you* stick your hand in?"

"Hey, you're the one who insisted on coming along for my protection." She folded her arms across her chest.

He rubbed the bridge of his nose. "Yes. What a terrible idea. Why do I never learn?"

"I'm just saying," she rationalized, throwing up her hands. "Berry never mentioned how much testing he'd done on this. Besides," she posed, tossing a resentful wave at the quantum shear. "When has going through one of them ever turned out well for me?"

Noah stifled his groan behind his hands in aggravation. He looked like he wanted to wring her neck. "For the love of god, Laney, can't you just—*oof!*"

Laney exhaled sharply, feeling the wind knocked out of her, short of blacking out, as she fell back on the pavement.

A man dressed in a generic office suit had come out of nowhere and tackled them both to the ground.

Noah grunted out loud, wrestling the guy off of Laney so she could scramble away toward the thicket for cover.

She gasped, her head snapping up in alert as Noah was pinned down by the man who was most certainly an agent from her own world's version of The Alliance.

It was just like Berry had said. And "they" had probably detected their quantum shear entry and sent someone to check it out.

Laney hissed in helpless frustration, looking around anxiously to make sure there weren't any more agents coming first. Not to mention, they were running the risk of someone else on campus hearing or seeing the commotion and waking up everyone.

She suddenly wished she had sneaked through some weapons from the other world. But it was too late now. All she could do was watch Noah struggle with the agent, rolling around on the ground.

"Noah!" she yelled hoarsely, trying to figure out how she could help him.

But Noah had a different notion.

"Laney—go—," Noah called out in a half-groan, even as he tried to break free from the agent's hold.

"What?" She looked shocked.

"Go!"

Laney panted as she looked helplessly between the quantum shear and the pair of them brawling on the ground. "I can't!" she maintained. "You'll be stuck here! Berry said—"

"Laney, go!" Noah yelled again.

Laney's eyes lit up as the Zeta device on her wrist began to beep in alarm.

The exit trace was fading away.

She swallowed hard. She felt frozen in her stance again. She wanted to jump on the Alliance agent to help get him off Noah, but the portal was about to disappear. This was her only chance.

"Go!" Noah's voice was nothing but urgent.

"Oh shit—," Laney cursed out loud before she took a deep breath and jumped into the quantum shear.

I O

Same

Laney crashed onto her bed, which she supposed would have snapped in two from the impact of her fall if not for the pile of laundry heaped on top of it.

She struggled to sit up and untangle herself from some clothes. "What? What am I doing here?"

She was in her dorm room, the sun was streaming in through the windows, and her bedside digital clock read *4 p.m.*

She checked the Zeta device. It did indicate that she was no longer in the previous world, except this other parallel world was uncannily similar to her own and somehow she had also jumped past the last sixteen hours.

But before she could analyze the Zeta device's readings any further, she heard footsteps at the door and clambered to hide under the bed just as she heard the door swing open and some people came in.

"Nope. Changed my mind. There is absolutely no chance

I'm going to be motivated enough to study this weekend. And if I take these home, they'll just sit on my desk, taunting me as they gathered dust."

Laney recognized the girl's voice.

"Don't worry, Laney," Darla responded. "We can always do another cram session on Monday morning. Besides, what else could we possibly be motivated to do?"

"I don't know about you but I have a triple trilogy and surround-sound home theater waiting. That's a little over twenty hours of space fantasy fun. My weekend's sorted."

There was some shuffling and thumping of things on tables before the two girls headed out and shut the door behind them.

Laney let out a breath in relief. That was close.

She couldn't help a little smile as she registered the fact that in this world, she and Darla were still the best of friends. Somehow, it gave her some reassurance that she was going to resolve whatever was going on back on her world, as surely what she had seen between her and Kevin must have merely been some kind of fluke, or an accident, or a hallucination, *something*.

What other explanation could possibly make any sense?

She crept out of her hiding place, keeping one eye on the door to make sure that the other her was not going to come in again.

Berry did say that any contact with her other self would have catastrophic consequences and jeopardize the mission.

Then again, the entire plan had already bombed.

She had left Noah behind in her homeworld. And now she was going to have to go on by herself.

She straightened up, squaring her shoulders. *You can do it, Laney.*

She'd told everyone that she could do this by herself. That she didn't need anyone to come along. She'd already survived this far. What was one more alternate parallel world and a supernova?

She chanted a mantra in her head, nodding self-assuredly to psyche herself up.

Child's play. Piece of cake. Walk in the park.

On her way out of the room, she walked past her desk and paused to fish inside a Hobbit hole figurine collectible. In her own room, she knew she kept some emergency cash in there. She grinned as she fished out a few coins and paper bills.

Sorry, other me, she thought. But this certainly qualified as an emergency.

Laney walked to the door and peeked out to make sure the hall was empty before she scooted out straight down the stairs to exit the dorms to go in search of the next traffic cone, which given the odds were, she figured, would also be at the paved walkway along the garden, beside the gym, on the way to the clinic.

She knew she shouldn't call attention to herself but as soon as she stepped outside, she couldn't help but marvel as she looked around. She must have looked as though she had never seen a school campus before.

The mid-afternoon sky was blue, dotted with white puffy clouds. The grass in the quad gardens surrounding the complex of campus buildings was the same green as her own world's. The faint but familiar sounds of students laughing and shouting and playing echoed across the football field.

When the school bell rang its last one for the day, her stomach fluttered at the sheer familiarity of the entire situation.

It was like she was home.

She swallowed. But she knew she wasn't.

She shook her head briskly to refocus. This wasn't her world and there might be Alliance agents lurking about waiting to capture her again. She needed to stay vigilant. And incognito.

She ducked her head slightly as she kept walking, trying not to look anyone who passed her by in the eye.

She was going to walk straight past the group of girls who were watching a group of guys playing ball when she overheard one of the girls giggle.

"Oh my gosh, Jake is so cute."

Laney stopped in mid-stride and turned to look toward the basketball court.

He wasn't hard to spot.

Jake Donovan. Every world's answer to "Hottest Hunk" in high school.

There he was, doing a fake and rebounding under the hoop, before doing a left-handed lay-up swish into the basket.

"And he's so good at basketball, isn't he?" one of the girls went on.

"He's probably good at lots of things. What do you think, girls?" another one remarked.

And the group erupted in girlish airy giggles again.

Laney had to roll her eyes, almost having to stifle her laughter in derision.

Jake and Noah were *so* different.

It was ridiculous to think about how she could have even mistaken one for the other in the past. And she was willing to bet all the stars in the cosmos that there was likely no way on *any* Earth that Jake was good at more things than Noah was.

Noah was like a jack of all trades. Except for he was also a master of all trades.

Her throat constricted sharply at the thought that Noah was no longer there with her. Despite what she'd said back at the sub, she knew for a fact, he was handy to be around. But she couldn't boomerang her way back to her homeworld to get him. Not just yet. She still had to find a supernova.

"Hey, who's the fan club?"

Laney blinked out of her trance and looked around. The rest of the girls had gone and she was all by herself standing by the sidelines of the basketball court, somewhat creepily watching the group of guys play.

She opened her mouth to try to formulate any lame excuse, sliding her glance past Jake, who was staring at her strangely, but her mind had gone completely blank.

Her face flushed red in embarrassment and she was about to whirl around to scurry away until she heard Jake call out.

"Hey! Have we met before?"

Laney tried to wave him away, quickening her pace.

"Aren't you the one who loves tomatoes?"

Laney froze.

What?

She was so shocked she couldn't move.

His question had her completely taken aback that it took her a few moments before she slowly turned to look again.

She narrowed her eyes at him. *What the damn hell...?*

His intense blue eyes met her gaze.

It was *Noah.*

But it was Jake.

It was Noah *pretending* to be Jake.

Laney couldn't believe what she was seeing. Her jaw dropped as she gave him a once-over. He was wearing the preppy sports jersey, the tailored pants, and his hair was slicked back off his face, instead of looking like a tornado had run through it.

He looked...ridiculous. *And* ridiculously, absolutely, incredibly super *gorgeous.*

Laney tried to get a grip and she shook her head briskly so she could try to respond. Her eyes widened slightly. *Oh crap.* What was that code word again? "Uhh...that depends, you know," she flustered. "It's all...relativity?"

Jake appeared to scoff to himself before he moved to walk to her with a casual wave to the others. "Gimme a sec, guys."

Laney could only stare at him, speechless, as he came closer, her mouth still hanging open.

Under normal circumstances, there would have been no earthly reason for Jake Donovan to ever in a million years approach her, so in another time and place, this would have all been very, very unusual.

But as soon as Jake figured they were out of earshot, it was like a shadow fell on his face and he shot her a flat, dark look.

"If I even hear one smart comment out of you about this outfit that I'm having to wear right now, I swear to god, I am going to boomerang home and strand *you* in this world."

Unfortunately, the look of intense displeasure on his face

was too much for Laney to handle and her façade of disbelief crumbled and she broke down into a fit of laughter.

"Holy crap, Noah. It *is* you."

Noah glared at her. He did not look happy.

"I'm s-so sorry," she wheezed, trying to get her giggles under control.

He looked more than a little curious, maybe even a little more than slightly displeased. "Didn't you recognize me?"

She still couldn't speak. She shook her head.

"Curious. Maybe only one primary can recognize the other at any one time."

"What?" she asked between gasps.

"Nothing."

She took a breath to collect herself. "Hey, so what the hell is going on?" she hissed in bewilderment. "You managed to make it through the quantum shear trace before it faded away? What happened to the Alliance agent?"

"I took care of him."

"You took care of him?" Laney repeated in disbelief. "That sounds exactly like the suspiciously convenient lie an Alliance spy would say."

"For the millionth time, I am not in The Alliance!" Noah rolled his eyes, exasperated. "I can't believe you still don't trust me after everything we've been through."

Laney huffed, making an obstinate face, but she didn't push her point. "Whatever. I guess we're lucky we both made it."

"Lucky? I can't even begin to tell you how glad I am to find you," he said, his eyes widening in displeasure. "I jumped into this world's Jake Donovan's parent's house hours ago and they thought I was him. So...so this!" He gestured to himself.

"Apparently, *their* son Jake was supposed to have left on a camping trip this weekend," he relayed. "Which he probably did. But when they saw me, they thought he had changed his mind and didn't go. I had to pretend to be him."

"So...this?" She gestured to his outfit while trying to suppress another wave of giggles. "Um, it really doesn't suit you."

He gave her a suffering look.

"Hey, Jake!" one of the guys from the basketball game called out.

Noah spun around, alerted.

"We're all going to The Shack," the guy beckoned. "So, are you coming? And...?" He looked over at Laney.

"Uh, yeah!" Noah yelled back with a nod. "She's coming too," he replied quickly. "This is Laney, my uh...girlfriend," he said, reaching over to awkwardly put his arm around her shoulders.

Laney shot him an incredulous sideways glance.

For a freaking genius, Noah sure didn't know how to behave around regular people. She was honestly surprised that he'd lasted this long without anyone noticing that he wasn't the real Jake Donovan.

Then again, Noah was a highly-skilled spy and soldier. He was probably trained to adapt to any hostile environment. Even a high school.

11

Camouflage

Laney leaned back against the wall outside the door of the boy's locker room, waiting, since Noah had insisted on changing out of his preppy clothes before they leave campus. She folded her arms across her chest, still trying to avoid catching the gaze of anyone passing by.

It was another one of those moments that she never thought in her wildest imagination was possible. Any uninformed passer-by would rightly assume that she was waiting to go on a date with Jake Donovan. Those passer-by's heads would probably explode if they knew what was actually going on.

Still, she had to check the little streak of thrill that coursed through her when Noah emerged from the doorway along with a puff of steam.

He had his usual flight jacket and jeans back on but he

had left his hair slicked back probably so as not to arouse any suspicion from his "friends".

He met her gaze as she looked him up and down in appraisal but she didn't say anything.

Noah rolled his eyes and dangled a set of keys. "You have to drive," he said. "I had enough trouble getting that infernal thing here by myself this afternoon."

Laney's eyes lit up. "You drove Jake's car to school?" And her expression which started as impressed turned incredulous. "What, you don't know how to drive a stick shift?"

He shot her a pointed look. "I grew up in Wellington. At most, everyone cycles."

She shook her head as she snatched the keys from his hand. In another time and place, Laney would have been thrilled to be able to drive Jake Donovan's classic Ford Mustang. However, the actual current circumstances were a bit of a damper. "Are we actually going to The Shack?"

"I've already done a preliminary sweep." He gestured to the HUD on his arm, not activating it. "The traffic cone is not on campus, which means—"

She was already nodding as they walked toward the parking lot. "We have to go out and find it."

"Do you know where this 'shack' is?"

"Of course. It's like the most popular dating spot near campus." She stopped short. "I mean, I know this isn't a date," she hurried to amend. "Of course. I'm just saying that's where normal students go when they go out on dates."

She bit her lip to shut up. *Alright, Laney. That's quite enough.*

Noah gave her an eyebrow-raised look but didn't comment.

Laney gripped the steering wheel as she drove down the tree-lined streets headed away from campus, her chest heavy with the feeling of impending doom as so far, things hadn't gone to plan at all.

For starters, they had already almost got separated. And with the portal marker not being where they were expecting it to be, it potentially meant even more delays in their already nerve-wracking tight schedule. She wondered when she would ever stop feeling on edge.

And being in Jake Donovan's Mustang with *a* Jake Donovan was just a smidge too eerie, it wasn't helping the situation.

Not to mention Berry's words that kept bouncing around in her brain.

Primaries... Fireworks...

She almost wished she hadn't asked Berry about it at all and stayed oblivious about what could have possibly been going on between her and Noah. She felt as though that "theory" was breathing down her neck like it was expecting her to do something, to feel something.

She shook her head to dismiss the thought. *That doesn't make it real.*

Besides, it was irrelevant. She already had a boyfriend. Or...she thought she did. She frowned at a sudden sting in her insides from what she had seen back on her world, but she shook it off again.

Regardless. Even if she didn't, even *if* Kevin was with Darla now, it was completely ill-advised for her to be starting any of this with Noah. She was going to go home soon. She was never going to see him again.

At least, not this one.

She sensed something was weighing on him too, even though his face was as sullen as it normally was. "What?"

Noah looked far away. "Jake's parents. They were similar enough to mine," he relayed softly. "I missed them."

Laney's eyes lit up in understanding. *Oh, of course.* She pursed her lips, not really knowing what to say. "That must have been rough."

He shrugged. "I know it wasn't them." He glanced over at her. "But it does get confusing. Doesn't it?" he prompted, a catch in his tone.

A corner of her mouth turned up as she gave him a quick sideways look as she was definitely one of the few people in the entire multiverse who would understand *exactly* what he meant, but she didn't say anything. She knew she didn't have to.

Noah gave her an appreciative look. Then he took a deep calming breath as though coming to peace with it as he settled to look out the window to watch the world zip by. "Dad offered to make me some crepes, which was weird because my mom was the molecular gastronomer—"

The car swerved across the centerline.

"Whoa!" Noah's gaze snapped to the wheel on which Laney's hands were not.

Laney, whose hands had flown up to press against both sides of her head, had her eyes squeezed tightly closed.

Noah's eyes lit up in recognition as his HUD beeped.

Laney was having another 'bleed through', similar to the one she'd had on the submarine yesterday, which was manifesting as her head feeling like it was going to implode. She screamed again.

Noah grabbed the wheel. "Laney! Stop the car!" he yelled, his face showing effort as he concentrated hard on not running the car off the road. "Laney, listen to me! Get your foot off the gas now!"

But she couldn't move. She couldn't think. There was nothing but intense pain.

"Laney!" Noah's eyes widened in dread as he saw that they were about to run head-on into something up ahead.

Laney was convulsing in her seat, her eyes beginning to roll back in her head.

"I'm sorry, Laney!" Noah called out before he flicked up his HUD and pressed a button.

Laney momentarily jerked in her seat before she fell slack against it.

Noah drew Laney up enough so that she couldn't reach the pedals before he pulled hard on the handbrake, making the car nearly spin out and kicking up a substantial dust cloud on the unsealed road as it screeched to a stop.

He collapsed back in his seat, still slightly heaving before he turned to check on Laney.

She was unconscious but breathing.

He swallowed hard, relieved, but unsettled. There was no way it was good for Laney to be receiving zaps from her CCL every time this happened. As it was, they would also be needing to find access to some type of laboratory with proper instruments to be able to remove the strip safely.

But first, they had to get moving again.

ASAP.

He patted Laney's cheek lightly, then started to shake her shoulder in an attempt to wake her, but as he did so, his gaze was distracted when the dust settled back around the car, and he looked around, entranced.

The car had swerved to a stop just before a fenced-off area with big red 'No trespassing. Quarantine zone.' signs all plastered on it, the area behind the fence so vast he couldn't sight where it ended.

He opened the door to get out, his gaze still pinned to the desolate expanse before him.

It looked like a bomb site or what would have been left of a populated suburb after a massive bomb.

The ground was dry, there was a smattering of dead trees along the road, the cracked bed of what looked like used to be a river, and ruins of structures crumbling in the dust as far as the eye could see.

Noah frowned, an image of his own troubled world flashing briefly in his mind.

"What happened here?"

He whirled around upon hearing Laney's weakened voice and jumped to support her arm as she straightened up from inside the car. "Are you okay?" he asked, his forehead creased with concern.

But Laney's mouth had dropped open. "What did this?" She squinted at the yellow police tape running across the street where it looked like the paving of the street itself cut off unnaturally at a certain point, just before the dark, barren land that lay beyond it.

He shook his head. "Looks like a bomb of some type," he guessed.

"A bomb," she echoed as they both walked up as close to the fence as Noah figured was safe to inspect it.

And as if on cue, the Zeta device beeped and Laney checked her wrist. "Oh boy."

Noah had already closed his eyes, wrinkling his nose in dismay. "Don't tell me," he started. "The orange cone is in there, isn't it?"

Laney nodded, looking dazed. "Uh-huh."

"Perfect."

***

Laney craned her neck briefly to read a road sign. "We just passed another county."

Noah who had insisted on driving was continuously scanning the road up ahead as they had been driving along the quarantine zone fence for about twenty minutes, trying to find a gate, a gap, or an entrance into the area with no luck.

Laney shifted in her seat with a slight moan.

He gave her a sideways glance. "Are you sure you're okay?"

Laney's head was still stinging from the aftereffects of the 'bleed through' and her CCL felt itchy but she tried to ignore it. "Fine."

Noah's forehead creased in concern again but he knew there was little he could do about it. He signaled to diverge at an interchange. "We should go back," he said. "Maybe we'll have better luck the other way."

She didn't reply. She was feeling exhausted, unenthused about either option. She gestured out the window after a few minutes. "I remember this used to be a wildlife reserve. And there should have been a country club over there, right before the interstate. It's so weird that it's all just gone."

"We need to find out more about this world so we know exactly what we're dealing with," Noah suggested. "Do you think the library at the school would still be open?"

Laney craned her neck back again as she spotted something across the road. "Look." She pointed out the window.

A big neon sign was blinking '*Open til Midnight.*'

The quarantine zone fence also ran right along a street that was across from The Shack. And when Noah slowed the car down, a voice calling his name made him turn to look.

"Hey, Jake!"

One of the guys from the basketball game earlier at the school was at the parking lot right outside the diner and spotted Jake's Mustang. He made a big wave to beckon them inside. "You finally made it! Hurry up and get in here, you sneaky lovebirds!"

Laney rolled her eyes. She would have found his comment annoyingly immature, except she was finding it refreshing to be around actual teenagers, with actual teenaged brains, with regular teenage concerns for a change.

Noah glanced back at Laney. "Feel like doing some recon?"

She shrugged. "I guess you'd better park the car."

The Shack was a fifties-inspired diner, with candy-striped window frames, shiny silver bar stools, lacquer tabletops, and pink leather booth bench seats, complete with a jukebox playing retro music. The place served thick milkshakes and some of the waitresses zipped around on rollerskates.

It was Friday night and the place was well close to crowded. Laney noted that a lot of the people looked familiar since they were also students from her school.

As they walked in, Noah gave a casual wave and a nod across the floor to the table full of jocks by the window where the guys he'd been playing basketball with were sitting with some cheerleaders, but he headed for two bar stool seats at the counter instead and Laney guessed that he wasn't so keen on continuing his masquerade as Jake Donovan.

Noah leaned against the counter. "Want something to drink?"

Her eyebrows rose. "You don't have any money," she reminded him.

He scoffed, looking miffed.

She handed him a laminated drinks menu. "I got it," she said, relieved she had grabbed some cash from her room. "Pick what you want."

"We're not here to drink."

"Then why did you ask?"

"I'm just trying to blend in," he rationalized, shaking his head. "I really don't understand this kind of world."

"I'm sure this kind of world doesn't understand you either," she quipped.

"We need to get more information about that quarantine zone. I thought I saw a newspaper box right outside. I'll go see if I can get one," he said, pushing off the bar stool.

Laney nodded, watching him go.

Noah passed a few girls on his way to the door and they turned their heads to watch him walk past.

One of them giggled. Another whispered to the others before very obviously gesturing at Laney, sitting at the counter. And then the three of them gave her curious, not exactly friendly looks as they walked past her on their way to a booth across the diner.

Laney had seen those looks before. Other girls at school used to give her the same looks when she had started going out with Kevin. It usually made her feel incredibly insecure, made her think she didn't deserve to be with him, made her afraid those girls knew there was someone else better for him.

She looked down at the empty stool that Noah had vacated. Somehow, she didn't feel any of those things right then. She shook her head to dismiss the thought. She wasn't really *with* Noah.

When she looked up again, she groaned as she could already see from the mirror behind the bar that two other guys were walking up to her from across the diner.

Both boys looked a few years older than her, and one of them, the one who looked like he was auditioning for a role in *Grease* later on, slid over to lean against the counter beside Laney with a wide grin on his face. "Hi there," he said. "I'm taking a poll for a local charity. We're concerned with the level of satisfaction of today's consumers. Tell me, are you satisfied with the service you've received tonight?"

The other guy who was hanging back was stifling his chuckle back as he watched his friend.

Laney didn't move, didn't look up. "Not interested.

Thanks," she replied with a tight smile. She was hoping they would just go away and leave her alone.

But "Danny" straightened up, his grin widening as he prepared to pose his next offer, putting his hand on her shoulder. "Oh, come on, don't you want to help out a—" And he broke off with a sudden yelp.

Laney looked up, startled.

Noah had grabbed his arm from behind, and was not-so-subtly, painfully, extricating it off of her. "Hey guys," he started, his face blank. "Why don't you go find someone else to annoy?"

The two immediately scrambled away. "Danny" was bent over, nursing his hand. It appeared Noah may have broken it.

Laney met Noah's gaze as he swung his leg over the barstool to sit beside her again. "Thanks?" she said, almost uncertainly. "We're supposed to be incognito, remember? I don't think you breaking that guy's arm is going to help that."

Noah grunted, looking away. "They were bothering you."

"It was fine—," she began to dismiss.

"Well, they were bothering *me*," Noah amended firmly.

She watched his expression, slightly amused.

Jake Donovan was not normally this intimidating. But Noah's spin on his personality was making him absolutely formidable. It was no wonder all the other guys in his world wouldn't even talk to her.

I2

Different

Noah crossed his arms, leaning his elbows against the counter, looking dissatisfied. "They were out of newspapers."

Laney narrowed her eyes in thought. "Or we can just..." She raised her hand to call the bartender. "Hey," she started with a sheepish smile, her gaze dropping to his nametag. "Paul. Could I possibly borrow the TV remote for one teensy minute? I really want to check on this reality show I'm watching."

The bartender looked to be in his early twenties, probably a college student on his part-time job. He simply grinned and handed Laney the remote control for the TV mounted up in the corner of the diner.

"Thanks," Laney said, already clicking on the channel button on the remote, settling on the next news broadcast channel she found.

Noah looked up to watch.

"Nearing the anniversary of the devastating global catastrophe. Commemoration event planned." was rolling along the bottom on the ticker tape as footage of quarantine zones, sinkholes, and more areas that looked as though a massive bomb had cleared it, like the one they had passed along the road, flashed on the screen.

She mumbled in surprise. "Well, that's different."

"It looks like this world has already suffered some side effects from a quantum spacetime disruption," Noah said, looking around as though re-surveying their surroundings in light of the new information.

"I thought you said this world was safe?" Laney asked through clenched teeth.

"It *was* safe."

Her eyes were still locked on the TV. "Oh shit, look at the date." She tugged on his sleeve. "Whatever it was that caused all this happened on the twentieth of March earlier this year. That was the day we first met, the first time I went through the quantum shear with you."

He shook his head ruefully. "Man, that event must have had some rippling effects throughout the spacetime continuum. That must be what Berry didn't want to tell us."

Laney's stomach was in knots. "I feel terrible. Like this is all my fault."

Noah didn't meet her gaze. "We both know whose fault all this really is."

She made a face as she also knew all too well whose fault it all was, but the fact that she was a 'Laney' too didn't appease her at all, especially since she had been an instrument in enabling it.

Who knew how many other worlds had been damaged because of her? How many more worlds were *going to be* damaged because of her?

"This doesn't change anything. We still need to find a way to sneak into that quarantine zone," Noah said.

Laney was trying to clear her head, but it wasn't every day that one found out they're responsible for severely damaging the spacetime continuum and it was difficult to refocus. She clenched her fists in remorse.

Noah's eyes narrowed slightly for a moment then he turned to Laney. "Do you like music?"

She blinked out of a daze and looked up at him in incredulous disbelief. "What?"

He met her gaze. "Do you like music?" he repeated before gesturing toward the corner, by the swinging glass doors entrance of The Shack.

Laney saw that he was pointing at the diner jukebox but it didn't explain his question. She shot him a strange look. "Are *you* having a 'bleed through'?"

He rolled his eyes. "Just come on and help me pick a song," he said, motioning her over.

"Fine." She hopped off the stool to follow him as he walked over to the jukebox. She fished out a quarter from her pocket.

Then Noah moved to whirl them around so that her back was to the jukebox.

Laney jumped, startled. "What are you doing?" she whispered.

He leaned his head closer. "Over my shoulder. Two o'clock. See those guys in the back?" he said under his breath, otherwise not moving an inch.

Laney discreetly glanced up over his shoulder to see the group of college guys wearing another school's letter jackets sitting at a booth almost obscured by a UFO catcher game.

"They've been following us since we left campus. I recognized their car when we parked. I'd seen it on the road when we were driving along the quarantine zone."

He'd spoken too near her ear that she felt shivers down her neck. "A-are you sure?"

Given that she'd been trying to avoid him for days, the last time he was this close to her was the night before she got abducted by The Alliance.

And even then, even when she didn't have a clue about the Primaries Theory, she'd already felt it. There was something about him. He didn't even need to touch her and she could already feel her skin tingling.

And it wasn't just that he was hot. There was just always something very reassuring about being close to Noah. A calm. A stillness. Of a foregone conclusion.

Noah met her gaze, only then realizing their proximity, and he registered the contemplative uncertainty on her face. Although instead of looking guilty and pulling away, like she had gotten used to him doing, he kept his electric blue eyes pinned on her.

"Don't worry," he assured huskily. "I wasn't going to kiss you."

She took a deep breath. She couldn't remember the last time she found freshly-showered soap smell so incredibly intoxicating. "I wasn't worried," she nearly stammered out.

It was getting difficult to stay upright, to not lean against him. But she caught the veiled amusement on his face. He knew exactly what was going on. And he had known right from the start.

And while in the past, Laney had ignorantly let herself get carried away by the unidentified compelling forces, this time, it had a more defined point that at least she understood.

But even so...

She couldn't look away from his mesmerizing gaze and was starting to heave.

It still felt...*inevitable.*

So what if the theory was right? More to the point, so what if the theory was wrong?

Noah's forehead creased slightly as he detected the apparent change in her conviction.

Laney's eyes trailed down the strong line of his jaw before her gaze was drawn to his mouth and she caught the hint of a smirk on his lips.

She swallowed hard, her heart pounding loud in her ears as she tilted her chin up the tiniest fraction of an inch.

Theories be damned...

"Laney?" Kevin's face appeared behind the window.

Laney jumped about a mile high. "Oh my god, Kevin!" She pushed away until Noah was a good three feet away, standing beside her.

Kevin pushed the swinging doors open, his eyes on her. He came in with three other friends, all of whom headed toward a booth across the diner, before he looked over to give Noah an exceedingly curious look.

Noah, obviously displeased, glowered at him in response but didn't say anything.

"Hey." Kevin leaned toward Laney, his one hand on her

shoulder to turn toward him, or more specifically, away from Noah. "What are you doing here?" he asked Laney, scanning over his shoulder to give the diner a once-over to see if she was perhaps with anyone else. "I thought you were having a girls' night in with Darla?"

Laney's throat was dry. "Uh..." Her gaze flickered up to Noah's, at a loss. Her heart was beating so fast, she thought she might have a heart attack.

"Hey. Jake." Kevin's greeting sounded vague, but definitely not pleased. "Nice jacket."

"I'm sorry. Who are you?" Noah's eyebrows were raised.

Kevin shot him an indignant look. "Uh, I'm Laney's boyfriend. We've been together for two years," he stated.

"Mm...I'm thinking it's only been like eighteen months." Noah narrowed his eyes.

Kevin's jaw dropped.

Laney cringed. "Kevin, hey," she jumped in, putting a hand on his arm before either of them could say any more. "It's okay."

He met her gaze coolly. "I'm sorry. I just didn't realize you guys even knew each other."

"Oh. It's fairly recent. Um..." Laney racked her brain. "We were just—just—working on a project together. A science project." That was actually valid.

Kevin put his arm around her shoulders. "Listen, it's getting pretty late. I'm sure Jake here has somewhere else to be. Why do you let me drive you back, huh? Get you home *safe*," he offered with a tone of authority, tossing Noah a casual glance.

Noah's expression was one of incredulity. "Are you implying she's not safe with me?"

"Noa—I mean, Jake," Laney cut in quickly. "Hey, um, listen, I really appreciate your help with the—thing but uh...I think maybe Kevin's right. We'd better do this later?"

Kevin smiled, already starting to walk away with her. "The guys and I just popped in for a root beer before game night. Why don't you come sit with us for a bit?"

"I still need your help, Laney." Noah's statement contained neither patience nor amusement with the situation.

Laney shot Noah a wide-eyed pointed look over her shoulder. *Be cool, man!* It wouldn't do either of them any good to blow their cover now. She motioned for him to hang tight as she was going to have to think of a way out of their predicament. And fast.

And three... Laney counted in her head, her jaw clenched in unease as she sat at the table, her eyes glued to the empty soda glass in Kevin's hand.

It was his third one. In fifteen minutes.

She put her hand on his arm. "Get you another one?"

Kevin met her gaze. "Thanks, babe," he said even as he moved to stand up. "But I gotta hit the head first."

Laney almost sighed with relief as she discreetly checked on Noah who had been sitting by the bar, his intense gaze glued to her for the last fifteen minutes.

It was like a nightmare, as the last thing she wanted right then was to have Noah watch her be on a "date" with alternate

Kevin, especially after the incredibly close call by the jukebox earlier.

But she furrowed her eyebrows when she found the particular bar stool empty. She scanned the diner to try to spot where Noah had gone, a slight frown of concern on her face.

Even though she was confident that he wouldn't have left without her, she was hyper-aware that they were on a clock, so as soon as Kevin had gone to the back, out of view, she also made an excuse to leave the table so she could look for Noah.

When Laney came around the corner, she tilted her head in puzzlement as she spotted Noah by one of the tables near the front. He was strangely enough, animatedly talking to a group of students whom Laney recognized were from the Science club at school.

"That's ridiculous. Look, even Einstein knew he was full of it," Laney overheard one of the students saying.

"Yes, but he did admit that the cosmological constant was his biggest mistake and yet it still became one of the biggest breakthroughs in scientific history, didn't it?" Noah was leaned against the back of one chair, dispassionately arguing his point.

Laney came up quietly and tapped Noah's shoulder. "Uh...*Jake*?"

He turned to look, his eyes still bright with fervor. "Oh, hey Laney," he began. "Would you tell these leptons that Einstein was an unequivocal genius?"

Laney cast a glance around the awestruck group, before returning her gaze to his. "Sounds *fascinating*."

Her use of the expression made him blink as though snapping out of a trance.

Noah looked around. The students at the table were all staring at him strangely, as for one thing, Jake Donovan had never interacted with them ever before. For another, he never in a million years would have been able to argue Einstein's theories so rationally.

Then again, he wasn't really Jake Donovan.

She tugged on his arm to steer him away from the table.

"Uh, Professor?" Laney quipped as she led the way toward the diner's exit. "Maybe you should limit your interaction with the natives. We're trying to keep you on the down-low?" She had a mischievous look on her face as she was reiterating Noah's own words to her from the airship last week regarding her interactions with the people from *his* world.

Noah shook his head in mirth as he opened the door for her.

"Now come on," she said, hurriedly leading the way back to his Mustang, already unlocking the car with the key fob in her hand. "I told those guys I was going to the ladies' and if Kevin knows me like I think he does, he's going to be looking for me in exactly eight minutes, by which time we need to be long gone."

Unfortunately, Kevin was a stand-up boyfriend, who just so happened to be getting something from his car too.

"Laney?" He looked taken aback when he saw her coming out. "Where do you think you're going?"

There was no one else outside the diner. No one else she could be coming out to meet.

Laney's brain blanked in panic for what could pass as a valid excuse for her to be going to take a ride in Jake

Donovan's car, not to mention for her to be having the keys to it right in her hand.

But Noah had had enough of delays. He tapped Kevin on the shoulder as he came up behind him, and as Kevin turned to look, Noah moved swiftly to knock him out, and Kevin collapsed in his arms, unconscious.

Laney watched in shock as Noah dragged Kevin toward his Prius and put him in the back seat. She caught the expression on Noah's face as he walked back to his Mustang and she shot him a dry look. "You enjoyed that a little, didn't you?"

There was a shadow of a grin on Noah's face but all he said was, "We should go."

13

Drive

"What's going to happen to him?"

Noah glanced up at Laney who had driven back to the main road that ran along the quarantine zone before asking her question.

"Who?"

"Kevin."

He rolled his eyes. "He'll just wake up in the morning with a little headache. I doubt he'll remember anything. Don't worry about him. He's a big boy. He's not even *your* Kevin."

The statement made Laney stop short.

Noah stopped too. "I'm sorry. That's not how I meant it."

She shook her head. "No, you're right. This is ridiculous. I just want to go home. And we're not even halfway there yet." Her dejected gaze flicked up to notice the traffic light turn yellow at an intersection and she stepped on the brakes to slow the car down.

Noah considered her expression. "Look," he started, sounding remorseful. "I'm sorry. I know how...important he is to you." He cracked his neck slightly while speaking. "But I promise you, whatever's happened on your world, for whatever reason, if given the choice, Kevin chooses Darla instead of you, he will have committed an error on a massive scale which he will regret forever."

Laney turned to stare at him, half-incredulous, half-terrified at the gravity of his tone.

After a moment, Noah's eyes softened as if he'd just realized how scary he'd sounded. He blinked, trying to sound casual. "I mean, you know. That would be totally lame."

She pursed her lips in amusement. It was very strange to be taking dating advice from 'Jake Donovan.' It was completely throwing her off.

"What?" He shot her a questioning look.

She reached her hand out to muss up his hair, completing his transformation back into Noah. "That's better."

He smiled, his gaze not leaving her face.

Laney drew a shaky deep breath, forcing herself to look away, just as the car behind them honked in protest and she looked up, alerted.

The traffic lights had turned green.

"Alright, alright," Laney mumbled as she slammed on the gas to get the car moving. She shook her head briskly to focus. "So do we have a plan?"

"Well," Noah started, peering out the window at the endless fence as they drove by. "If the quarantine zone is what that news report said, then at least we know the public will have been warned to stay away from it. We won't have to worry about witnesses. But given that we still haven't found a gap in the fence, we might not have a choice but to cut through it."

"You said you thought the fence was electrified," Laney reminded him. "We don't have any tools or gadgets."

He shrugged. "I might still have one or two tricks up these vintage sleeves," he said with a catch in his tone.

She chuckled in dry mocking.

Then Noah's eyebrows furrowed. He leaned over to check the side mirror before discreetly looking over his shoulder to see behind them.

"What is it?" she asked, checking the rearview mirror herself.

He was already groaning. "I think we're being followed."

Laney moaned in annoyance. "No!"

"It must be those guys from the diner," he guessed. "Did you recognize them?"

She grumbled. "I can't believe we're being chased again."

"Hey, at least we're not on foot this time."

"Oh, yeah, this is much better," she said as she floored the gas.

The black sedan car following them started to gain speed too.

"Yup, they're definitely chasing us." Noah's arm was braced across the back of the seat as he kept an eye on the car trailing behind them. "They must be Alliance."

She tilted her head. "Or maybe that guy whose arm you broke is looking for payback," she quipped.

Noah's face was straight. "Or it's your boyfriend's friends looking to pick a fight."

"Oh boy." Laney blew out a breath at those odds. "Come on, Alliance," she said, crossing her fingers.

She checked the side mirrors again in time to see the other car catch up to drive alongside them, right before they sharply maneuvered to attempt a sly sideswipe.

Laney spun the wheel quickly away. "Whoa!" Her pulse started to race.

Noah was trying to peer into the other car but its windows were all tinted heavily. "I can't tell who it is."

Laney bit her lip in concentration, shifting gears and pulling away to get some distance from the other car again. "Well," she said, furtively looking around the road up ahead. They were headed into the residential area along the old lake. "Whoever you are, let's see if you know this neighborhood as well as me."

"As well as *I*."

"Shut up, Noah!" she snapped.

She revved all three hundred and ten of the horses in the engine and the car all but flew down the road with a roar, just before she jerked the wheel to make a screeching right and then an abrupt left, zipping the car neatly into a little grove in the middle of two pastel suburban houses before shutting off the engine and all the lights.

Laney was still heaving when she saw the other car zoom past, missing them completely. She grinned in triumph, only then turning to look at Noah.

He was staring at her, the expression on his face what must pass for awe. "Been in many car chases before?"

"No, but I do watch an unhealthy amount of movies."

"How do you even know about this place?" He looked

amazed as he inspected the grove that was sheltered under overgrown vines and shrubs.

Laney replied offhand. "Are you kidding? This whole area used to be farmland. It's full of shady little corners. It's become sort of a best-kept secret place for kids to—" She broke off, realizing what she was about to say.

She met his expectant gaze and blinked to rephrase. "Hang out. And talk. All night."

"All night?" Noah's face was skeptical.

"If they wanted to," she added tentatively. She was probably the last person on Earth who should be trying to explain the grand young tradition of "parking" to Noah.

He scoffed in mocking. "I feel like I almost need to double-check if you're having a 'bleed through' right now."

Laney's shoulders shook in mirth. But she knew fairly well he didn't need to check. Noah was the one person who could recognize her no matter what for some reason.

Or perhaps for one very specific particular reason.

As the silence fell between them, Laney felt the familiar probing warmth in his gaze again. Her pulse raced in the recollection of what had almost happened at The Shack.

She supposed she should have been relieved that Kevin had come at that exact moment but she couldn't help feel as though she'd been left hanging.

Her stomach twisted at the stark reminder of another certain Kevin whom she should have been thinking about instead. Not to mention a certain fiancée of Noah's whom he didn't even know was actually not entirely lost.

Damn that damn theory.

She fidgeted in her seat.

"What is it?" Noah noticed her unease.

Laney's gaze was fixed to the dashboard. "Berry told me."

Noah's eyebrows rose in a silent prompt.

"About primaries."

If he was surprised, he didn't show it. "It's just a theory."

She met his gaze again. "I know."

Noah studied her expression, trying to read what her vague response meant. His forehead creased as he leaned toward her slightly. "I mean it's not like we don't have a choice. Like we can't control it."

"I know."

"And we don't have to do anything we don't want to."

"I know."

After a quiet pause, he turned back to face forward in his seat, his tone changing to add, "And you're going home soon."

"I know..."

She studied his profile. He looked like he was having an internal struggle himself and her heart began to pound again. Connection or not, she was certain they were both thinking the same thing.

It would be fighting a losing battle any way anyone looked at it.

I can't believe you still don't trust me after everything we've been through...

The fact of the matter was it was easier not to fully trust him. It was easier to think that he was a bad guy. That way, she could more easily rationalize her choice to stay away. It was likely the last thing stopping her from falling into that trap.

Alarm bells rang in her head.

Home. You have to go home.

She shook her head briskly. *Focus.*

But Noah seemed to be on the same page as well. He cleared his throat, piercing the silence. "We need to get back to the quarantine zone," he said, his tone reverting to authoritative.

Laney nodded and she looked up to check the road to make sure it was all quiet before she propped her hands on the steering wheel again. "That should be enough time."

Noah looked at her briefly before he turned to watch the back of the car as Laney reversed out of the grove.

Only as soon as they had returned to the main road, they heard a screeching of wheels, and the same car from before appeared on the road behind them, along with its friend: other identical suspicious black sedan.

Laney checked the mirror irritably. "What? How do they keep finding us so fast?" She floored the gas again, heading away from the suburbs.

She wasn't really a car racer and she was going to run out of moves before this world ran out of bad guys. Their only hope was to find the quantum shear exit trace and get out of the current dimension.

She looked up ahead as the features on the roadside changed from rows of houses to uninhabited wild green bushes, providing quite the contrast from the dry, brown desolation of the quarantine zone right across the street.

After a moment, Laney spoke up. "You said we'd need to cut through the fence."

"Yeah." Then his eyes lit up as he easily realized where Laney was going with her statement.

She gave him a sideways glance. "What do you think? Do you think it'll work?"

Noah was already busy checking to make sure both their seatbelts were clicked on properly. "I think maybe you've gone a little bit nuts. But yeah, that would do it."

Laney revved the engine again, watching in the mirrors as she got some distance from the other car. Then her gaze flickered up at the next stretch of quarantine fencing, making sure the area would be as isolated as it could be.

Noah braced his hands on either side.

"Here we go!" Laney gripped her hands on the wheel, steeling herself for the impact as she quickly veered the car to the left, jarring over the roadside gravel as they careened toward the high fence.

But instead of giving way or crumpling back to let the car through like Laney hoped it might, the reinforced steel fence merely bent to wrap around the front of the Mustang as it smashed head-on, making the car come to a full stop.

Laney coughed through the smoke, whacking away the deflated airbag and already beginning to undo her seatbelt before she noticed that Noah was unconscious and was bleeding from the side of his head. *Oh shit.* "Noah?" she called, tapping on his shoulder lightly at first, then harder. "Noah! Wake up!"

The sound of other roaring engines made her sit up in alarm. She glanced over her shoulder to see the cars that had been chasing them weaving closer into view.

"Oh no. Noah, come on!" she yelled in his face, but he didn't respond. She looked up and down the road anxiously. There was no way in hell she was going to be able to carry his unconscious freaking hockey player figure to be able to run or hide.

She was going to have to leave him. Again.

Laney flung the car door open and moved to go but her hand froze on the door latch. She knit her eyebrows, heaving as she wavered for a moment. If she left him here in his condition, The Alliance would definitely get him. But if she didn't, The Alliance would get them both.

After another second of indecision, she groaned out a curse before turning back into the car. "Noah! Dammit, wake up!" She patted his cheek even harder, short of slapping him.

And when he stirred, Laney breathed a huge sigh of relief as she flew around to his door to drag him out of the car, putting his arm over her neck and shoulders as she labored to make their way through the gap in the fence.

I4

Gravity

Laney had a feeling that the six gargantuan guys hopping out of the two black sedans were merely dressed like college students. She tried to move faster but it wasn't easy supporting Noah along. "Oh no—"

All at once, she felt someone pull Noah away and someone else grabbed her arm, hooking an elbow around her neck. "Agh!" She squeezed her eyes shut in pain.

But before she could gag or try to struggle away, the next thing she knew, she was hoisted up onto something and she felt a sudden rush of wind all around her.

And after a few moments, everything went silent.

Laney opened her eyes, her expression of dread transforming instantly into amazement as she looked around to find that all six goons were passed out on the ground around the cars.

Noah, his eyebrows furrowed in alert and wakefulness,

had scooped her up and climbed on top of one of the black sedans before deploying whatever it was that had incapacitated everyone.

She looked up at him with an almost knowing expression. "Do I even need to ask if that was one of Berry's weapons you sneaked through?"

Noah smirked as he set her down. "Let's go." He motioned for her to jump off the car. "Those guys are not going to be passed out for long," he informed her before making a break for it through the quarantine fence.

The fog was rolling in, giving the night and the empty desert a spooky feel, but Laney shook it off as she struggled to keep up with Noah's long strides.

His eyes were locked on his HUD as he pressed on. "I'm getting readings from right up ahead."

Laney glanced down to check on her Zeta device as she ran to follow suit.

The device had begun to beep faster pulses in an indication of how close they were getting to the portal location.

"We're almost there," Noah noted.

Laney tried to catch her breath, looking up ahead in eager anticipation.

"There's the orange cone!" they both said at the same time.

Laney and Noah looked at each other in surprise as they had pointed in two different directions.

She squinted to see more clearly in the dark and her jaw dropped again.

That entire area of the quarantine zone was littered with an assortment of orange cones.

"Oh no."

Some of the orange cones were tattered, even crushed, or flattened, even as some were pristine and looked almost new.

Noah raised his HUD to analyze the two orange cones closest to them.

"Jeez! How many Laneys have been through this world?" Laney looked bewildered. "They can't all be portal markers."

He frowned as he read the data. "Nope. They all are," he told her. "Some of these cones are reading as having come from miles away. Could be that another side effect caused by the quantum event has made them all converge in this location."

"Well, hey, if they're all portal markers, let's just pick one and get the hell out of here ASAP," she began, moving to walk toward one.

Noah caught her arm. "I'm also reading some erratic gravity readings throughout this area."

Laney keyed off the word "erratic" and she froze, her expression turning wary. "That doesn't sound good."

Noah pulled her along as he stepped back. He bent down to pick up some stones. Then he flung one toward the nearest orange cone before it zoomed straight down with a crunch, piercing through the ground like a bullet, making an actual hole.

"Whoa!"

He flung another toward a second orange cone and this time, the stone catapulted straight up into the air.

"Watch out!" Laney covered her head as she tried to watch where the stone would land. She peered up at the sky. "Hey, where did it go?"

"This must be why this whole area is fenced off. They didn't want anyone to come any closer." He threw up his hands. "It's a freaking gravity minefield."

"*Seriously?*"

He turned his attention back to his HUD. "Stay close. I'll map the gravity fields as they form."

Laney held on to Noah's arm as they navigated the gravity minefield to approach an orange cone for assessment. She winced as she started to feel droplets of rain falling from the sky. "What—?" She looked up and was going to complain again until she noticed the effect of the gravity fluctuations on the rain. There were some spots around them where the rain didn't fall and the ground remained dry.

"Give me your hand," Noah's voice cut into her reverie.

Laney raised her wrist so that Noah could analyze the Zeta device readings.

"Something's wrong."

Laney grumbled, already annoyed. "Of course it is."

Noah ran his hand through his hair, shaking off droplets of water. "The exact vibratory coordinates for the next world on the chain won't resolve. Or maybe some of these cones only accept certain trajectories..."

He moved to lead them both carefully toward another orange cone to try again. "It's still not working," he groaned. "I can't isolate the exact position of the next world."

"Oh, *come on!*" He yelled out in aggravation as another cone failed to match and they approached yet another orange cone.

Laney looked down at the Zeta device on her wrist in helpless dejection then out of the corner of her eye, she noticed several orange cones seem to stir.

But Noah was doing some magic on his HUD and Laney's ears perked up at the familiar sound of the wind rising as a result of the forming quantum shear.

"Wait, I think I have something—," he began.

"Stop, stop." She grabbed his arm. "Stop that for a sec."

She gestured to a couple of orange cones which she could then visibly see were slowly, inexplicably, moving on their own. "Are you seeing this?" she asked, a bit of dread creeping into her tone.

He consulted his HUD for a moment before his expression darkened.

"What?"

He moved toward another orange cone. "We have to get out of here now."

But she held him back, warily. "What's going on?"

Noah looked hesitant to explain. "The exit trace we're trying to open," he started. "It's disrupting the electromagnetic levels in this entire area. It looks like all the gravity wells are trying to converge. And if all the gravity wells come together, it's going to become a single massive event."

"A black hole?" Laney had to raise her voice to be audible as the rain had begun to fall harder.

"And it's going to swallow the whole state and who knows what else."

Her eyes widened in alarmed devastation.

Was she about to destroy this entire state? This entire world? Was she going to ruin the lives of every living being here too just so she could go home?

Noah read her expression. "I'm sorry, Laney, but we need

to get a move on. You don't want to be here when that happens."

Laney blinked through the rain, her heart almost stopping.

No. That was Eleanor.

Eleanor was the one who didn't care about ethics and morality and was willing to sacrifice everything to advance her own goals.

Unless... Laney felt sick to her stomach. Was she Eleanor now?

"I've got it!" Noah exclaimed all of a sudden.

Laney swallowed hard in remorse. "Wait—" Except when she stepped back, she felt the rain stop falling completely and her eyes popped open in recognition. "Oh no shit—!"

The gravity fluctuation had shot her up into the air in an instant, and the next thing she knew, something tugged on her arm. She looked down in amazement.

Noah had abandoned the forming quantum shear and somehow shot a rope up from his HUD from the ground to latch on to her. She looked up to see that the rest of her was flailing upward into the dark sky.

"Hold on, Laney!" Noah called out.

The wind was whipping rain sideways into Laney's face and she felt the upward pull of gravity increase and Noah's rope began to slip off from around her muddy arm. She struggled to grab the rope with both hands, before looking back at Noah again, horrified distress written all over her face.

But his gaze was pinned on his HUD. "Hang on! The gravity fields are about to shift again," he yelled out.

"Help me!" Laney cried out, breathing in short gasps, holding on for dear life as she also didn't want to catapult into orbit either. Her heart pounded in her chest. "It's getting harder to hold on!"

Noah was pulling hard on the rope. His eyes widened as he felt the ground shake from underneath him, making him lose his footing, slipping in the mud for a second. He looked around as the trembling continued. "Oh no."

Laney looked on in horror. From up high, she could see several massive networks of cracks appearing on the wet ground across the quarantine zone, accompanied by a loud rumbling, as the shaking continued.

Without warning, the upward tug of gravity on her ceased and she began to hurtle back down to earth. Her scream caught in her throat. She squeezed her eyes shut in anticipation of the pain as she fell from some twenty feet in the air.

But it was a shorter fall than she expected.

"*Ohh—*" She still groaned from the impact. She opened her eyes and looked around. The earthquake had caused parts of the ground to plateau. It was still quaking beneath her as the ledge kept rising. She peered over the edge to see Noah down a thirty-foot drop, across what looked like a six-foot-wide canyon that was being gouged across the desert, with several orange cones and chunks of earth crumbling and falling into its dark abyss.

"Noah!" Laney was panicked.

The earthquake had knocked Noah on his back. He managed to get back on his feet and looked up to follow her voice. His eyes were urgent. "This world is about to collapse!"

"No kidding!"

He squinted through the rain, consulting his HUD again, his forehead creased in deep thought. "Laney," he began out loud after a moment. "You're going to have to jump to me." His statement was punctuated by a flash of lightning.

Laney shot him a look of disbelief as she struggled to get up. "Are you crazy? There's no way I can jump across this."

"Laney, you have to. I'll catch you. Don't worry."

"Don't worry?" she echoed, aghast. "Don't tell me not to worry. That's a stupid thing to say."

The ground trembled again and Laney fell on her knees.

"I'm tracking a gravitational anomaly. I'll jump up to catch you, Laney," Noah explained, sounding frustrated that he couldn't elaborate further. "There's no time to explain the math right now."

"Math?" She looked incredulous. "What does math have to do with anything?"

"Look, just—when I say 'now', you have to jump across to me, okay?"

Laney's stomach turned as she stared into the dark depths of the chasm between them. She was surely going to fall into it. She couldn't figure out what the hell was going on in Noah's brain. She was heaving as she straightened up, struggling to keep her balance. Was he really making her jump off a cliff?

Noah glanced down at his HUD briefly and when he called out to her again, there was a hitch in his tone, mixed in with confident reassurance.

"Trust me."

Laney's gaze snapped to his and the look in his eyes silenced her doubts.

Because she understood. Because she knew.

She swallowed hard, getting ready.

"NOW!"

And Laney leaped off the cliff.

15

Feedback

"Ohh!" Laney fell on top of Noah and the two of them sprawled on the floor.

Noah coughed out a groan, squeezing his eyes shut to recover from the quantum jump. He was probably having difficulty breathing with Laney's entire weight on him restricting his airflow but he kept holding on to her as though it was a force of habit.

They were both still soaked through from the rain.

But they were indoors now. Somewhere.

Laney's head shot up with a gasp, almost already in distress over whatever threat their new surroundings posed.

The hallway was dark, deserted.

She could just make out what looked like shelves or trolleys parked alongside a corridor of closed doors. The place smelled like alcohol and formaldehyde that Laney figured they must be in some sort of hospital.

She took a deep breath in an attempt to stop heaving.

Despite it looking as though they were safe for the moment, she was still having trouble willing her pulse to settle down since she had just almost fallen into a dark chasm to her death.

If Noah hadn't managed to hitch a ride on a gravity fluctuation to catch her and then open up a quantum shear exit trace at the exact right moment, Laney figured they both would have been done for.

Even in the faint light, she easily met his gaze when he opened his eyes again and she couldn't help a nervous, extremely relieved chuckle.

"I can't believe we made it," she remarked in awe.

A slow smile spread across his face as he looked up at her.

Her gaze distracted to where her fingers were involuntarily stroking his hair and she furrowed her eyebrows. "Oh."

She couldn't seem to stop touching his hair, the sides of his face.

He didn't stop her either.

Her heart began to pound in her chest, and when her eyes met his again, there was no mistaking the intensity in it. His stormy blue eyes were practically searing into her.

"I thought I told you to stop saving my life all the time," she chided softly, a slight jest in her tone.

Noah's arms tightened around her in response, his voice low. "Last time I promise."

She could feel his heart pounding in his chest against hers even through his clothes and she felt a warm shiver course through her. Her fingers grazed his bottom lip as her gaze dropped to it.

It wouldn't have taken much. She only needed to dip her head a couple of inches for her lips to catch his. Even less when he lifted his head to willingly receive her.

BEEP! BEEP! BEEP!

Laney jumped, startled, instantly pulling back.

Noah groaned in acute displeasure, his head falling back onto the floor and he muttered a sharp curse. "Whatever the hell it is, ignore it," he told her, the roughness in his voice resembling gravel.

She gave him a pointed look as she pushed up off of him. "It's from the Zeta device, Noah."

"I don't care if it's from a weapon of mass destruction right now. That timing sucks."

She bit her lip from the fiery look in his eyes. Honestly, she was disappointed too. And for the first time, she didn't feel any regret or remorse about their almost kiss.

It was incredibly liberating.

She cast him an amused smirk. "At ease, soldier."

He chuckled in his throat.

She moved to settle cross-legged on the floor to check the device on her wrist. "Hmm." She curled her lips. "That's weird. There's something wrong with this. Looks like it's on the fritz."

"What?" Noah sat up, alerted, an instant crease of concern on his forehead. "Show me," he beckoned her over so he could inspect the device. His face blanked. "That's not good."

She wrinkled her nose as she tapped on the Zeta device's garbled screen in an unsuccessful attempt to clear it.

Then she heard Noah curse again.

He was checking his own HUD, an irritated frown on

his face. "Dammit. That last jump must have damaged my HUD too."

"Oh." The hairs on the back of her neck stood up in ominous apprehension. Without their devices, it would be near impossible to find the next exit trace or even to figure out where they were.

"Where do you suppose we are then? What is this place?" Laney scanned up and down the hallway again.

But Noah was still grumbling over his broken HUD in extreme aggravation, and Laney figured, despite its origins, to Noah, losing his HUD must have felt as though he had lost an appendage.

She squinted enough to make out a window to a room across the way. "Hey." She tapped on his shoulder. "Look. An office."

"So?"

She rolled her eyes. "So if you stop crying over your broken toy for two seconds, maybe you could try to take a peek inside and see if there's anything useful in there that might tell us where we are. You know, a company logo, a stationery header, a postage-paid envelope," she supplied, half in mocking.

Noah blinked at her, snapping out of his daze. He looked almost surprised at her reasoning, but he just sneaked toward the window and craned his neck to look. His posture eased as he found the office empty, only to immediately stiffen again, his eyes widening in flat dread.

"Oh no."

"Oh no, what? Where are we?"

He signaled for her to come up to the window. "Look *when* we are." He gestured to a calendar propped on top of a table.

Laney checked the flip calendar and her blood ran cold. Then she looked up the brass clock that was mounted on the wall inside the room as well.

"Oh. No."

20th March 2020 was the date.

8:55 p.m. was the time.

She looked around. "Do you think—?"

He was already nodding. "Yup. We've gotta be at GNR."

Laney made a retching noise. "Perfect."

"Well, the good news is, at least we know exactly where we can locate a quantum shear exit trace." He looked around, trying to recognize by sight in which part of the lab they were.

"Do you know how to get to the jump platform from here?" she wanted to know.

"I guess we'll find out," he replied, straightening up.

She straightened up herself, but before she could move to brush past him, he stepped in her way, standing almost close enough to her that she could feel his warmth. She looked up at him expectantly.

His gaze on her was heavy with unsaid words. "Listen, Laney..." he began under his breath.

It was enough to make her stomach flutter but then he lifted his hand to touch her cheek and her heart skipped a beat.

She covered his hand with hers, giving him a small smile. "I know." She acknowledged with a nod. "We can talk later."

His eyebrow rose in suggestion. "Talk?"

Another streak of thrilled anticipation shot through her

but she just waved for him to get going. "Come on, Noah," she teased. "Don't you remember? Time is of the essence."

He smirked and motioned for her to follow him down the hall.

Laney tried to make out the strange shadows and shapes in the dark hallway. So far, she didn't recognize anything, so she figured they must be in a completely different part of the humungous lab complex.

The creepy feel of her surroundings brought her back down to reality and her anxiety intensified as she registered the actual gravity of the situation.

"I can't believe we're back here," she said, her face sullen.

"There's no telling where we are," Noah supplied with a solemn tone. "It may just be a different alternate dimension that just so happens to have the same lab, the same standard-issue GNR coffee mugs," he drawled. "The same bake sale fundraiser." He pointed to the cupcake poster on the bulletin board before nonchalantly gesturing to the small window to the outside that they passed by. "The same interdimensional invading force assembled outside."

"Oh boy."

"Either way, we have to be careful. Good thing I still remember where the guards would be posted. We really can't be caught this time," he pointed out. "The last thing we're going to want to have to deal with right now is a time loop paradox."

"That doesn't sound good. What is that?"

"Never mind," Noah dismissed. "I just want to get the hell out of here ASAP."

"Ditto. This place gives me the heebie-jeebies." Laney rubbed her hands over her arms.

He looked at her. "*That* doesn't sound good. What is that?"

"Never mind." She smirked in mocking. "I just mean I have really bad memories of this place."

A shadow crossed Noah's face and he looked away. "Me too."

Laney stopped short as she realized what he meant. "Oh shit. I'm—so sorry. I shouldn't have brought it up."

Noah looked like he was a million miles away. "You won't believe how much badgering Berry had to do to make me agree to dismantle the quantum jump platform to build the smaller form factor." The struggle was obvious in his tone but he tried to joke about it. "We'd worked for months trying to reverse the effects of the energy wave that had taken Eleanor. But I understood." He pursed his lips. "We had to make sure that the new version wouldn't be capable of sending the multiverse into oblivion again."

Laney watched as a tortured expression flashed across his face. It was as though he was reliving the past eight months of his loss in his mind.

There was an unexpected constriction in her chest and she wanted to kick herself for stirring up those bad memories.

But there was a strange look on Noah's face when he spoke again. "I have to admit it took a while for me to accept the fact. You know...that Eleanor was gone."

Laney made a face. She almost felt the silence that followed choke her, as it was a stark reminder of the secret that she had promised Berry she wouldn't tell Noah. And it was beginning to burn a hole in her conscience.

She cringed in tension. "What if she's not...? Gone, that is."

He narrowed his eyes at her, almost in ridicule.

"What if...you *could* get Eleanor back?"

He shot her a look. "What do you mean?"

And she caught the brief spark that flickered in his eyes.

That was his hope of being reunited with Eleanor—his long-time girlfriend, his actual fiancée, the Laney from his own parallel world with whom he could *actually* be.

For a split second, Laney felt a strong wave of jealousy, possessiveness, and confusion. And she chickened out. "Um, nothing," she mumbled and she turned to keep moving so she wouldn't have to look at him.

Noah watched her in puzzlement.

But before he could say anything, there was a concentrated bright glow around the corner and he winced, alerted, motioning for them to press back against the wall as he crept forward to investigate.

Laney followed cautiously behind him but then it dawned on her exactly what could be glowing at the end of the hallway.

It appeared that she and Noah had found themselves in a hallway that led to some scaffolding that overhung a very familiar scene transpiring below.

"Oh god," she breathed in recognition. "It's happening again."

It almost felt like she was watching a show. Not counting the handful of lab assistants operating the machinery and the soldiers, Laney recognized the four main characters in the scene.

Off to one side was Noah, being held at rifle-point

by three faceless military goons. The megalomaniac General Blakely was holding onto Eleanor's arm as they stood beside a control panel. And then there was a Laney, who was trapped in the quantum jump platform receptacle as she was about to be used as some type of energy conduit.

No. It wasn't a show. It was real.

Laney vividly recalled the helpless, terrified, panicked sensation she'd felt from being trapped in that godforsaken platform receptacle. She tried to shake the feeling off, even as her heart was already pounding in distress.

She looked up at Noah, but his face had an unusually curious and strangely wondrous expression on it. "What is it?"

Noah murmured, "She's still alive. I can save her."

Laney thought she'd misheard. "What?"

But Noah went on, almost eagerly. "You were right. She's *not* gone yet. There wasn't enough time to save her before, but now there's two of me. *I* can save Eleanor."

She shot him a look of incredulous disbelief. "What? Noah, no! That's not what I meant. You heard what Berry said. We're not supposed to have any contact with our other selves. It could jeopardize everything."

"*Could*," he echoed. "Or maybe Berry was wrong and nothing's going to happen."

Laney couldn't believe what she was hearing. "No! You said it yourself, remember? There's some things we shouldn't mess with," she reminded him.

But Noah was quick and stealthy. Before Laney even noticed, he had started to move down the ladder toward the ground level.

Ohh shit. Laney hissed out a curse as she had no choice but to follow suit, hoping that everybody else would be otherwise preoccupied to notice the two of them climbing down the side of the huge hangar lab.

As soon as Laney was close enough to the ground, she jumped off the ladder to catch up to Noah who was marching straight toward the quantum jump platform.

"Noah, stop it!" she whispered hoarsely as she pulled on his arm, tugging him back into the darkness behind the corner wall.

"Let me go, Laney. I have to do this."

Laney tried to meet his gaze, her grip on his arm tight. "Think about it, Noah," she implored. "We have no idea where we really are. This might not even be the same parallel world. Even if we save her here in this dimension, it still won't change what's already happened on yours."

"You don't know that!"

"Noah, you're being totally irrational. Snap out of it!"

"I said let me go," Noah insisted.

Blakely's laughter rang in the air.

The sound made Laney's stomach turn.

It was almost time.

Noah was struggling even harder against her, trying to break free.

Just then, a bright violet light illuminated the entire lab.

Noah's eyes were full of urgency. "That's the kickback. I have to save her!"

"Noah—NO!" Laney cried out and with all the strength she could muster, she grabbed and very nearly slammed him back against the wall to pin him against it.

His eyes were ablaze with the light when she met his gaze.

"Eleanor has the lo-jack necklace!" she yelled in his face at the same time that Blakely's scream rang in the air.

"*NO!*"

Noah's eyes widened at her statement and he instantly stopped struggling.

But Laney squeezed her own eyes shut, turning back to bury her face in Noah's chest. She didn't want to watch everything happen again.

Noah clenched his jaw as he put his arm protectively around Laney, his heart pounding, and all he could do was watch as Eleanor and Blakely's images got dissolved by the quantum jump platform energy wave all over again.

And all the power in the entire lab facility, across the thirty kilometers between France and Switzerland, went out in a blink, accompanied by all the lab staff's moans *Oohhh* in unison.

And after a few minutes, everything was quiet again.

16

Compensate

She should have known. She *did* know.

Even Berry had told Laney that Noah would be obsessed with getting Eleanor back. And given the opportunity, Noah would take it every single time.

Laney's face felt hot and she couldn't help the sharp stinging in her chest even as she clutched at Noah's shirt.

She pulled away slightly, sneaking a look up at him. She was dreading what she would find in his eyes.

Noah was standing frozen, a seemingly shattering degree of remorse in his eyes.

Laney clearly remembered how devastated he had looked when he had lost Eleanor the first time. She couldn't even imagine what it must be like for him to have to go through those emotions again. Especially since he had an opportunity to save her this time around. She'd always had a feeling he had regretted which one of them he had saved.

She was right.

Incredibly loyal. That's what Maia had said he was.

Noah would still do anything for Eleanor. She was the one he truly loved.

Laney stepped back from him, a deep furrow on her brows. "I'm sorry."

But she told herself she had done the right thing. Of course she had. They couldn't risk any more damage to the spacetime continuum than there already was.

She blinked in the recall of just the previous parallel world they had been to and what may have happened to it as a result of their opening up another quantum shear to escape.

There was another one of her in that reality. And another Darla. Another Kevin.

Normal people living their normal lives. And it was highly conceivable that their entire alternate world had just been sucked into a convergence of gravity and could be no more.

Because of her.

She shook her head, almost feeling sick.

Because of *her*, Eleanor had been lost to the quantum shear eight months ago. Because of *her*, every alternate dimension she'd ever been to had been irreparably damaged and/or was possibly gone completely.

Now she was getting all hung up over someone else's fiancé. And all this despite herself already having a boyfriend.

Had a boyfriend?

Her chest tightened. She couldn't even recall one single thing she'd done in the past week that was of any virtue.

To think, she'd spent all this time worrying about what if

Noah was the bad guy, when the truth was that *she* was the bad guy.

She watched the other pair of Noah and Laney recovering by the other side of the disabled quantum jump platform.

Her heart pounded in her chest as memories of that particular exchange flooded her senses.

It seemed so long ago, even though it had only been a few months.

She couldn't possibly have imagined at the time what was in store for them next. So much had happened since.

And yet...

There was a lump in her throat as the same realization struck her again.

She hadn't belonged there. And she hadn't belonged with him.

She still didn't.

The other Noah and Laney finally straightened up to leave the lab.

Laney's eyebrows were still furrowed when she looked back at the Noah beside her in the shadows. She took a deep breath, as though finally reconciling with the truth and she regarded him with a plain look. "Are you okay?"

Noah met her gaze and somehow recognized the concession in her eyes. "Laney..." he started, already intent on explaining.

"It's fine," she dismissed, dropping her gaze and taking another breath. "I totally understand. Eleanor was your fiancée. You love her. You've always loved her. Of course you wanted to save her. I'm so sorry."

He clenched his jaw again.

"And I'm sorry I didn't tell you about the necklace. When you get back to your world, you can work with Berry to try to get the Laney you love back," she suggested with an encouraging shrug before moving to walk toward the quantum jump platform. "Now, let's better do this before those soldiers wake up or before the other you comes back."

He caught her arm again. "Wait. Laney. You don't understand," he stated. He gave her a pointed look as though in incredulity of how she could still possibly doubt him. "It wasn't love. It was..."

"What?"

"Guilt."

She narrowed her eyes at him in question.

Noah sighed after a moment. "The truth is, I wanted to save Eleanor because..." He shrugged a little. "Because I knew, even if I had to make the same choice again, I would have always saved you." He looked pained from holding back but there was no escaping the truth.

Laney's stomach churned but she shook her head, almost in mocking. "Noah, we both already know how this is going to end. We're going to find the supernova and then I'm going back home. That's the mission."

Noah's expression darkened.

"I'm displaced," Laney reminded him. "We are *literally* from two different worlds. We're not supposed to be together. We're not even supposed to have met."

He came closer, almost leaning over her. "But we did meet. I found you," he replied fervently. "I *literally* went to the ends of the world to find you."

"Well, you shouldn't have." She stepped back, giving him

a half-devastated look. "I don't know what I was thinking. I'm not supposed to be here. For god's sake—" She threw her hands up. "None of this would have even happened if I hadn't got shot. If I hadn't come with you in the first place..." she trailed off, her eyes clearing after a moment as something clicked in her head.

Noah looked up, noticing her dazed expression. "What?"

"Oh my god."

"What?" he pressed, almost impatiently.

"Noah." She met his gaze. "The quantum jump machine is right here," she murmured her incredible epiphany. "I can undo everything."

His eyebrows furrowed. "What? What are you talking about now?"

"Send me back," she repeated, a look of urgency in her eyes. "Send me back to that day. You told me the small-scale jump platform couldn't do it, but we have the big one right here, right now!" She let out a short, jubilant squeak.

"You're serious." Noah studied her expression. "Laney, that would mess with spacetime even more. That's exactly what Berry didn't want to have happen."

Laney threw up her hands. "This is different! This is *better*," she argued. "You can send me back to the day we first met and I can make it so that I never even get shot in the first place! Don't you see?" she implored. "Eleanor would still be alive. P.T. would be fine." She shook his arm. "Noah, the world we'd just come from, it wouldn't have all got sucked up into a black hole. None of the horrible things I've done would have ever happened!"

Noah was already frowning. "You couldn't have known

back then what was going to happen. And we didn't have a choice in that last world."

"Didn't we?"

Noah shook his head. "No." He tilted his head slightly to regard her desolate expression. "Laney, you have done nothing wrong."

"But Eleanor—"

"Is *not you*," he finished, his tone firm. "You can't punish yourself for something you didn't do," he began in earnest. "The best thing you can do right now is to keep going and...maybe someday you *can* fix it."

Laney still looked unconvinced, her gaze dropped in dejection.

Noah tipped her face up. "*We'll* fix it," he pledged with a resolute determination. "You need to remember, you're not alone in all this. Whatever happens, I'll be here for you." His tone changed. "Besides, even if you did go back, there's no guarantee things won't happen exactly as they already have," he pointed out. "You don't know things might turn out even worse."

That made Laney scoff in mocking. "Worse than this?"

"Yes." He braced his hands on her shoulders. "Laney, I don't want to lose you. And I know it may not seem like it now, but from the very first day we met—" A corner of his mouth turned up. "I wouldn't change one minute of it."

After a beat, she shot him a half-incredulous look. "Not one minute?"

He cracked a small smirk. "Well." He amended meaningfully, "Maybe one."

Laney couldn't help a chuckle, but she couldn't pretend

his apparent attachment to Eleanor earlier didn't sting and it was still fresh in her mind. She resisted the urge to make a face. "What about Eleanor?"

A shadow flickered across Noah's face. "It's great that we can get her back," he admitted. "But you know how I feel. And what I'm feeling, it's not for Eleanor." He moved to cup her face in his hands. "It's for you," he declared. "It always has been. Not anyone else. Not any other *version* of you. Just you." He shook his head again. "I know I shouldn't. Believe me, I tried everything not to. But I don't want to keep pretending anymore. Do you?"

His blue eyes were intently searching hers. But she could tell from the urgent tone of his voice, he wasn't so much asking the question because he didn't know the answer than he was wanting to hear her say it out loud.

Because he already knew the answer.

Laney blew out a breath. "This is such a bad idea," she mumbled in exasperated ridicule. "I'm supposed to be going home."

"What if you didn't?" The urgency and tension in his tone were palpable.

She looked stunned at his question. Then she started to heave, almost in disbelief that she was even considering it. What would her parents say? She would never see Darla and Kevin again.

Laney stared up into his eyes. It always felt like he could see straight into the depths of her being. But was she prepared to leave everything and everyone she knew behind for him?

When she didn't respond right away, Noah's face fell for a second. "I'm sorry. I didn't want to put you on the spot.

You don't have to answer that." He dropped his hands. "And I...understand if you feel your connection to Kevin is too strong. I know I'm nothing like him," he said, his voice low. It was obvious he was trying to keep the jealousy out of his tone, but it wasn't working.

Laney's chest constricted at his expression. It was as though she could feel his desolation, his frustration. She could feel it deep within herself, mirroring her own emotions.

He was right. He was nothing like Kevin.

He was more.

A soft groan came from somewhere behind them as some of the soldiers were waking up.

Noah glanced over in alert. "Oh. We have to get out of here." He motioned Laney toward the jump platform.

"Noah," she began. Her chest felt full and there was another lump in her throat. She felt overwhelmed with anticipation and promise and resolution. She wanted to tell him everything.

He gave her a small smirk. "It's okay, Laney. Hold that thought."

She met his gaze with a reassured smile.

Noah tinkered with the control panel for a few seconds and looked up with a self-satisfied nod when a swirling vortex of doom formed upon the platform. "Target coordinates are locked in," he noted, then raised his eyebrows. "Shall we?"

Laney stared into the menacing mouth of the black hole again before indicating a short nod.

And they both stepped through the quantum shear.

17

Jump

"Laney? Laney!"

Laney heard faint voices in her reverie but she was having trouble opening her eyes.

"Dek, do you have them?"

"There's some kind of interference. I'm trying to clear it up."

She groaned, still in a haze.

"Oh no. Someone else is trying to get them."

"Hold on, Dek. I'll help you focus the transmission."

"Trin, I'm losing them. The shear is dissipating. I'm losing—"

***

"K-drive disengaged."

"Thanks, Sigrid." Trin's tone was calm, collected. Her entire crew of The Dauntless had probably done space fold jumps over a dozen times before and were already accustomed to it.

Meanwhile, Laney blinked hard. She had to hold her hand over her mouth to dispel the urge to throw up.

But when she looked up at the main window, her nausea was instantly replaced with wonder.

The ship was coming up behind an asteroid-like small moon, where just beyond it, Saturn's magnificent rings bathed in the golden yellow glow of the giant gas planet, hovering in the big black void.

It was definitely a far cry from the planetarium show.

"Wow," Laney murmured.

Dek grinned from the seat beside her. "Haven't you ever seen Saturn up close before?"

She shook her head. "Nuh-uh. In my world, we've only ever sent unmanned space probes this far out in the solar system."

He furrowed his eyebrows. "But you guys made it to the moon and Mars, of course?"

She pursed her lips. "Nope. Just the moon. The entire space program sort of fell apart after that."

He whistled. "On our world, after the Apollo missions, the space initiatives just took off—pun definitely intended," he quipped. "And it's been a steady journey to the stars ever since."

"You're lucky." Laney craned her neck, narrowing her eyes at the view, even as she was still belted into her chair, but all she could see was Saturn and a few moons. "Where's the generation ship?"

"We're still about a half an hour away from The Aquila," Dek replied. "We couldn't risk coming out of K-jump right on top of it."

"Cam, status," Trin called out.

Cam consulted the several screens before him, pressing more buttons, before replying. "We're good, Commander. I'm not showing that The Aquila has detected us."

"Good. Keep our profile low," Trin instructed. She pressed the communicator button on her earlobe. "Sol, keep your finger on the button in case we need to rabbit."

"Aye." Sol's voice came over the PA.

Laney furrowed her eyebrows, looking at Trin and Dek in turn. The tension seemed to have risen on the bridge but she couldn't tell why.

"Sigrid, what's the current solar output of Betelgeuse?" Trin spoke up.

"Current solar output of Betelgeuse is at four-hundred percent."

Trin nodded. "Start the timer." Then she swiveled around in her chair to regard Laney with a stern look. "Last chance, Laney. Are you sure you understand what you're doing? You might not be aware of this but cosmological phenomena don't tend to wait for anyone."

Laney took a deep breath, taking in Trin's full meaning.

It was highly likely that she was going to miss the supernova altogether. She was going to miss the only window for her to be able to get back home. She was exchanging Noah's life for her own.

She swallowed hard and nodded. "This is the best idea my non-genius mind can come up with. I mean, I'm not the famous Dr. Laney Carter," she added, offhand.

Dek looked to be in deep thought. "Who's that?"

Laney looked shocked. "You've never heard of Dr. Eleanor Carter?"

He shook his head. "No. At least, not in our world. Sigrid?" he prompted, glancing up.

"There is no known record of an Eleanor Carter being born on Earth or any other off-planet colony."

"Wow. This is definitely a different universe then," Laney mused.

"Are you sure, Sigrid?" Trin followed up.

"You can check for yourself, Commander. Shall I print all seven-point-five-nine billion birth records out for you?"

Laney stifled her laughter as she met Dek's equally amused gaze.

Just then, the bridge panels all lit up in bright red while a loud alarm blared on the PA again.

Trin sighed, exasperated. "Sigrid, would you give it a break?"

"I am not kidding this time, Commander. I am detecting three Alliance ships on an intercept course."

At that, Trin's eyes lit up in alert as she spun her chair back around.

"Confirmed," Cam verified. "Three Alliance scout ships about two minutes out."

"So much for the element of surprise. Sigrid!" Trin yelled

out. "Prepare evasive maneuvers." She shook her head. "I'm suddenly regretting not getting that weapons upgrade last year."

"I told you—"

"Shut up, Cam!" she snapped then tapped her ear communicator. "Sol, stay sharp. This might get a little rough."

"What is it? What's going on? Are you guys in some kind of trouble?" Laney looked back over at Dek expectantly.

He gave her a sheepish smile. "The truth is The Alliance is looking for us too."

"What? Why?" Laney looked stunned. "I thought you guys were scientists?"

"Well, this *is* a science vessel," Dek replied. "We study stellar phenomenon. That's how we made contact with Berry a few years ago. We were already monitoring the red supergiant when we happened to catch one of the frequencies Berry was using for his experiments."

"Here they come," Cam announced, his tone grave as he watched his screen.

Laney jerked in her seat as The Dauntless made a sharp maneuver to avoid the scout ships.

"As you can probably tell the discovery of another parallel dimension is an incredibly big deal in the scientific community," Dek went on. "They don't use the term, but technically, The Alliance has flagged anything extradimensional as 'forbidden' and therefore illegal."

"They can do that?"

"Cam, can you bring us closer to that patch of asteroids?" Trin instructed, pointing to about two o'clock of the ship.

Dek tilted his head to give Laney a look. "I'm not sure

what you know about The Alliance, but they're pretty much the government. They used to just advise governments on scientific matters then at some point in the last few years, they took over entirely."

"Why?"

"We're not sure." He shrugged. "When they found out about our contact with another dimension on the monitored feeds, they told us to shut it down and surrender all our findings—"

"But you didn't."

"But we didn't."

"And now they're looking for you."

"You got it. They don't know which team the report had come from. That information has fortunately been lost."

"Ahem. Hacked," Cam interjected even as he frowned in concentration over his console.

"Right." Dek nodded. "Still. They're really cagey about anything not from this universe. We'd all be toast right away if they detect our black hole radio or *your* presence. I've heard there's even a standing bounty for anyone who surrenders trespassers from alternate dimensions."

"Yikes."

"I can't shake them, Commander," Cam replied. "We're not going to be able to evade them for much longer."

"You don't have any weapons at all? Space torpedoes? Projectile cannon thingies? Nothing?" Laney looked at each of them.

"This is a research vessel," Dek reminded her pointedly.

Then Trin turned to meet Dek's gaze. "Dek, do you remember that time on 'Proxima b'?"

Dek responded with an instant brief nod.

Laney blinked. "What's that?"

He reached down to activate his magnetic boots and un-did his seatbelt before unclipping Laney's.

"Whoops—" She floated up off her chair.

Dek grabbed her arm like a balloon string and guided her back through the bridge doorway to the corridor. "This way."

Laney could still hear Cam and Trin yelling in the bridge as they tried to prevent a full-on space battle which they would no doubt lose. She swallowed. "Dek, what happened on 'Proxima b'?"

He merely winked at her at the same time pushing a button on a panel by the wall and a sliding door opened with a whoosh before he nudged her squarely in the back to shove her into the little capsule. "Happy landings," he bade with a small wave.

Laney whirled around in time for the door to slide closed in her face and she was thrust against the wall as she felt the capsule eject from the Dauntless. *WHAT THE—?*

She heaved in alarm as she tried to peer out the window, but the motion of the escape capsule was making her woozy, and all she saw were the three Alliance scout ships closing in on her position, and then The Dauntless disappearing in a blink, before she passed out.

18

Anomalies

"Oh, you've got to be kidding me!" Laney could already feel the tug of something restraining her wrists before she even opened her eyes to find herself in a small interrogation room, her wrists and ankles strapped to a desk chair with duct tape

There was a sleek curved table before her, the usual mirrored panel in the off-white walls, the single light fixture on the ceiling, and the door with the little glass preview window.

She tried to squint through the mirrored panel even though she knew it was pointless to try and determine if anyone was on the other side. But as it was, she was all by herself.

Laney blew out a breath. *Well. Things could be worse.*

She thought of The Dauntless, slightly annoyed. For all she knew, they could be cashing in on that surrendering the trespasser from another dimension business.

She groaned. And it probably served her right for being all gung-ho about mounting a big rescue mission, putting everyone else in jeopardy again for her own selfish reasons. She wasn't trained for any of this. She was neither a genius scientist nor a super-secret spy. She was a laughably-average high school student.

She frowned and struggled in her chair, trying to figure how much movement she could still make in it. Then she peered at her wrists closely and then bent over to see if she could bite through the tape, growling at it in the effort. She was almost grateful they weren't metal restraints.

But as she was leaning forward, she tipped over in the chair, almost falling face flat onto the table, if not for how she'd suddenly gotten up on tiptoes, with the chair attached to her back instead of her being stuck in it.

Her eyes widened in delighted relief as she realized she could slowly move to tiptoe back away from the table. Her eyes looked to the door eagerly.

Unfortunately, with her next few steps, she tripped and fell on her knees, before the weight of the chair made her sink on the floor altogether.

The door opened with a shush.

"Impressive."

Laney couldn't see who it was but she mumbled, trying to move her head up off the floor, "I'm glad you think so."

She felt herself being lifted off the floor, her chair put upright with a thud, before she met the girl's gaze.

She didn't look much older than Laney. She had red hair and was wearing a type of jumpsuit uniform similar to the Dauntless crew and a wry look on her face as she surveyed Laney's appearance, while two men wearing nondescript business suits and earwigs flanked her.

"Is it Miss Carter or Dr. Carter? How's it going?"

"I'm sorry. Have we met before?" Laney asked, trying to be vague on purpose. She wasn't entirely sure what they knew about multiverses, but she figured it was better to be safe than sorry.

Except for the girl's next statement confirming it. "As a matter of fact, I have met another one of you before."

Laney blinked, stunned. *What?* That made no sense whatsoever. The Dauntless had confirmed that there was no other Eleanor Carter in this parallel world. So how could this girl possibly claim that she'd already met one?

Unless...

Laney stopped short as it clicked.

Oh, Eleanor. You are one sneaky mad scientist.

Berry had even suspected as much. Somehow, and for some strange reason, Eleanor had already been to this parallel world before and didn't tell anyone.

"Red" waved dismissively with a low chuckle. "And before you deny it, we already know you're from a parallel world," she said. "Our instruments have confirmed it. Just like that other boy."

Laney's pulse began to race. "Where's—where's Jake?"

"Oh, don't worry about him." Red looked up and signaled a nod to the two guys, both of whom promptly turned to leave. She perched herself to sit upon the corner of the table. "You know," she began as soon as they were alone. "I'm not usually involved in these—interrogations. So there must be something really special about you for them to have brought you to me." She paused to consider. "Or something really *wrong.*"

Laney glared at her. "Who are you? Why am I here? Where's Noah?"

Red tilted her head, amused. "I thought you said his name was Jake."

Laney bit her lip.

But before she could say anything else, the door opened again and a young man wearing a white lab coat came in, carrying a silver briefcase.

"Ah, Verren. Perfect timing," Red remarked.

Laney stiffened as Verren came up to her.

He plunked the briefcase open onto the table and Laney could see he had several tools inset inside. He picked up one of them then moved to employ something against Laney's neck, something that pinched.

"Ow." She winced. "Hey! How about gentle next time?" she suggested irately.

Verren didn't flinch. He applied the tool onto the surface of a tablet device that he was holding. "Hmm..." He murmured as he was reading. "They were right. We can't use her."

Red raised an eyebrow. "Interesting. What about the other one?"

Verren nodded as he put the tablet back in the case. "Him, yes. He may be just exactly what we've been waiting for to get our breakthrough."

Red gave him a self-satisfied look. "I told you we were close. Aren't you glad you didn't apply for that transfer yet?" she quipped. "Three-point-five-billion dollar money pit my ass."

Verren gave her a teasing jeer. "Let's just say my expectations are way lower than the committee's, *boss*. You know they only care about results, especially with this program."

Laney watched them warily. "What are you two talking about? What breakthrough?"

Red answered her question with a question. "Did you know that all matter vibrates? That's simple physics," she dismissed offhand. "Everything from the same dimension vibrates with the same frequency."

She went on with a small wave. "Well, guess what? You and your friend are obviously not from this dimension." Then she regarded her with a look. "Tell me, Miss Carter. Where are you from?"

Laney glared up at her, her tone dull as she replied, "Florida."

Red chuckled again, low and throaty. She walked across the room and when she pressed a little button on a wall, the mirrored panel cleared to display some type of surveillance video feed.

Laney peered at what was being shown on it. A large board had been pushed up to the "camera". She was surprised to see that the board had a similar geometric shape diagram drawn on it that was on Berry's "peanut map".

But at the same time, they all heard a loud groan of pain as the button that Red had pressed must not only let them see what was on the feed but also hear it.

"What was that?" Laney's eyes widened in dread.

The yelling didn't stop.

She winced. "Is that Noah? What are you doing to him?"

Red looked at her calmly, gesturing to the map on the screen. "See, we've already determined which dimension your friend is from," she called out to be heard over the noise then gestured to Verren. "But we can't seem to find where *you* came from. Your readings are all fuzzy."

She glared at Red, her stomach turning over at the blood-curdling sounds of pain from the other room, from what was undoubtedly Noah. "What's happening to Noah?" she pressed.

Verren was still standing beside Laney and he reached out to tilt Laney's head to one side. "What's this?"

Red glanced back. "What is it?"

Uh-oh. With all the rush to rescue Noah, Laney had forgotten that her CCL was still attached.

"There's something installed under her ear," Verren replied, training another one of his tools toward it. "They must have missed it down below. A monitoring gadget of some type. It looks like it's from the same dimension as the other one." He whacked the bottom of his palm against his device a couple of times, shaking his head. "Sort of. It's also a bit fuzzy."

Laney was heaving, her fists all balled up. Every scream of pain from Noah was gutting her insides.

Red watched Laney's face intently then after a moment she straightened up and pushed the button again, making the mirrored panel come back and the room became silent once more. She turned to the door. "Cut her loose."

Verren looked up at her, surprised.

Red looked somber. "Whatever she is, I don't think she knows either."

He looked dubious for a moment but then he finally shrugged and reached over to cut off the duct tape around Laney's hands and feet.

Laney looked as though she was going to vault up from her seat. "I want to see Noah," she demanded.

Red rolled her eyes, her hand on the open door. "Yeah, yeah, let's go." She beckoned her over.

Laney shot Verren a wary look as she moved to follow suit, rubbing her sore wrists.

But as soon as she stepped out the door and into the hallway, her jaw dropped in awe. She couldn't help but walk up to the window to marvel at the view.

The Aquila was the biggest *anything* Laney had ever seen in her life. She was in a structure along the curve of a massive spaceship made up of two spinning concentric circles. From the window, she could see a couple of ships approaching to dock onto the inner ring. Just beyond the outer edge, she could still glimpse Saturn and its glorious rings amidst the black void of space.

Looking up, Laney had a one-eighty-degree view of hundreds of people going about their day within the different levels of the shiny generation ship along the huge outer ring. There were large terrarium gardens, green forests, man-made lakes, and there were austere-looking building structures, as well as what looked like tidy sections of housing communities. Various robots, automated machines, and a sleek transportation network, all gliding smoothly, traveled on the narrow rails along the annexes connecting the habitats.

"Exactly how many people are on this ship?" Laney wanted to know.

"About fifty thousand, give or take a few."

"Holy wow..." she mumbled, still gawking.

But Verren nudged her forward to follow Red down the hall. "Keep moving."

Red had paused beside a doorway. She swiped her hand on a sensor panel to activate the door.

Laney gave her a suspicious look. "Where are we going?"

"Down to the lab to see your boyfriend," Red replied.

"He's *not* my—," she began to protest but before she could throw her hands up in helpless dismissal, the door slid open, revealing a spotless white capsule shuttle that had wide windows and two benches fitted on each side.

Laney thought it looked half train car, half elevator, and figured it must be how the fifty thousand people got around within The Aquila.

Verren motioned for Laney to get in and sit down.

"Put your seatbelt on," Red told her. "We wouldn't want you to float away."

19

All Wrong

Laney felt almost sick to her stomach from the changes in gravity they encountered on the tube ride and was relieved when they finally got off.

The Alliance was holding Noah somewhere at the very core of the generation ship. There were fewer windows in that part of the ship and everywhere was wall-to-wall white panels.

They passed a large door that was just sliding closed and Laney craned her neck in wonder as she glimpsed what looked like a dozen smaller spacecraft parked in a large hangar, at the end of which you could see a huge open port leading straight out to space.

But before she could look some more, Verren was back beside her, nudging her forward again. And the feeling of panic spread through Laney as she moved to follow Red, leading the way toward another set of doors.

Laney rubbed her hands over her arms.

Red glanced back at her, the expression in her eyes strangely interested.

"What?" Laney shot her a pointed look.

She dismissed offhand. "Nothing. You seem cold."

Laney narrowed her eyes. "What's it to you?"

"This ship is completely climate-controlled. The temperature is never lower than seventy-two degrees," she noted casually. "It's just odd," she remarked before the door shushed open and Laney heard the scream again.

"Noah—" She tried to hurry to push past Red to see but Verren held her back.

"Hey!" Red whistled, waving her arm to signal the two lab technicians standing behind a control panel. "Let's give our friend a bit of a break, shall we?"

Laney looked around. The laboratory they had walked into must have been at least ten times the size of what she could see since large plastic sheets were hanging from the ceiling to obscure what was past all the control panels, and when one of the lab technicians left the area, he walked past one of the sheets, revealing a small peek at a much bigger space beyond it where there were even more labs and people in white coats working on other machines.

Verren pushed Laney forward and her breath caught in her throat.

Noah was strapped to a solid vertical slab, beside a table where his jacket and all his belongings had been dumped. He looked exhausted, his hair matted against his forehead. But she could faintly see his chest moving. He was only passed out.

Laney sighed in relief. "Noah."

"He's fine." Red insisted with a wave as she walked over to

one of the machines spewing out paper with readings and line graphs on it. "See?" she prompted. "In fact, he's showing a 99th percentile rank in his frontal lobe faculties. It's almost off the charts!" she commented brightly. "I would be very interested to study this brain up close."

"What are you doing to him?" Laney was still trying to struggle her arm away from Verren's grasp.

"Just some tests," she replied as though it was anything other than the invasive, painful procedure it was. "Hey Verren, have you seen this? There's something weird going on with his blood work. I mean this DNA analysis is all kinds of exciting."

Verren dragged Laney along as he approached the console where Red was to study the chart with her. "It's got an accelerated degradation pattern."

"So the brave must indeed die young. It must be unique to his dimension." Red turned to Laney. "Tell me, did some type of apocalyptic event occur in his world too?"

Laney chewed on her bottom lip, trying to rack her brain for a way to help out Noah or to escape herself, but she was stumped.

Red snapped her fingers in the air. "Hello? I asked you a question."

Laney jumped with a start. "Y-yes, uh," she began, meeting her gaze with a nod. "Yes. A global cascade bomb wiped out most of the population."

Red raised an eyebrow. "Huh," she huffed. "I guess in that respect, our world got off a bit lucky."

"Lucky?" Verren mumbled with a cynical scoff. "It's not the word I would use."

That caught Laney's attention. A feeling of dread was creeping into her stomach. "What happened to your world?"

Red shot her a narrow-eyed look, and when she spoke again, there was a hint of contempt in her tone. "A few years ago," she began. "There was an interdimensional breach at the LHC labs in Geneva."

Red's lips curled up as she acknowledged Laney's stunned look. "You guessed it," she said. "It was you—the other you. And that little blip triggered a massive chain reaction. Weather anomalies, tsunamis, earthquakes, sinkholes the size of football fields. It made Earth basically uninhabitable." She gestured ceremoniously around them. "So here we are."

Laney groaned inwardly. *Great.* Eleanor was like the freaking gift that kept on giving.

Red tilted her head as though in melancholy. "You know, The Aquila was the first generation ship ever built. We've been in space now for over ten months. And we're never going back." Her expression darkened for a moment before she shook her head briskly, looking up to meet Laney's gaze again. "So you'll understand if we're a little apprehensive about interdimensional trespassing."

Laney swallowed. That incident must have been what caused The Alliance in this world to stop merely advising the government and take over.

Red stepped back, reaching up to tug one of the large plastic divider sheets aside. "Look familiar?"

Laney gasped. "Oh my god."

It may have looked like a scale model in an opaque rectangular box, but with the same machine components made entirely of glass and mirrors, it was unmistakable.

Red's team had built their own quantum jump machine.

Laney followed a lead from the machine traveling through a spaghetti wire mess on the floor, almost already knowing that she would find the other end hooked up to Noah's slab. "Oh shit." Her voice hushed as Red's plan cleared in her mind. "You're going to use Noah as the grounding wire."

Red's eyebrows shot up in surprise. "Ah, she's much cleverer than she looks, folks." She glanced over at Verren. "Verren, can you set up another molecular vibration analysis? I want to re-run that test on her. Make sure the guys didn't miss something before we move on. And then—" She smirked as she walked up to Noah. "I want to see more of this amazing little gadget that's integrated into his arm."

Laney's eyes widened.

"That's an impressive level of human augmentation right there," she said, peering closely at his arm. "Shall we see how it responds to certain stimuli?" she suggested with a Dr. Frankenstein glint in her eyes.

And Laney felt sick. She piped up loudly. "Here! Here, why don't you analyze this? Study this." She gestured to her watch. "This is called a Zeta device. It will let you travel across dimensions. Just please, stop whatever you're doing to him," she pleaded.

Red shot her another surprised look. "Really? You're willing to give up your little wonder gadget?" She shook her head. "If that is what you say it is, I don't think you realize what kind of advantage you'd be giving us."

Laney stuck her chin up. "He would do it for me."

Red let out a light laugh.

"So here, take it!" Laney held out her arm emphatically.

She exchanged a look of ridicule with Verren before she went on. "I think we're good on the gadgets so we'll pass. Besides, that could be a trap and I need to ensure that we protect ourselves from the threat of your worlds."

"You're the threat." Noah's voice was gravelly but the defiance was clear from his tone.

Laney's eyes lit up. Noah had regained consciousness. "Noah!" She tried to pull away to go to him but Verren held her fast.

"*And* he's back." Red rolled her eyes. "Mr. Had To Be An Asshat and almost killed three of my men."

"Are you okay?" Laney called out to him, worriedly searching his face.

Noah merely coughed in response.

Laney turned to Red in frustration. "Just tell me what you want from us."

Red looked cynical. "Want? We don't want anything from you."

"Then let us go!" Laney insisted, giving her an imploring look. "Look, you don't understand. I have an—appointment. And if I miss it, I'll never get back home."

"Honey." Red gave her a fake sympathetic look. "Bigger picture. This doesn't just concern you." Her tone was firm. "You're not going anywhere. You're staying right here."

"Stay?" Laney mocked. "You want me to live here? On the generation ship?"

Red blinked. "Oh, no, no. Sorry. I meant in our detention cell." She waved in ridicule. "We couldn't let you run amongst the population and potentially contaminate it."

Verren let out a chuckle at how she could have possibly thought otherwise.

Ahh...much better. Laney resisted the urge to roll her eyes. She glanced up at Noah in anguish then she looked up at the guy with the vise-like grip on her arm.

Verren's face was cold, closed.

Laney could sense that he was brimming over with bitterness. It wasn't unlike the expression Noah usually wore when asked about his homeworld and she guessed something devastating must also have happened to him as a result of the disruption in spacetime. It was clear there was no dissuading him from his convictions.

Laney bit her lip and turned back to Red again. "Please." She didn't know what else to try. She took a long shot. "I'm just like you," she started. "I'm trying to right a wrong, trying to set things right—"

"LOOK AROUND!" Red whirled around, cutting her off, so loud she made Laney wince. Her eyes blazed in anger, betraying the cool and calm façade she had been effectively representing as she gestured around them. "This is what's wrong! This is what interdimensional breaches have done to us! We're not the bad guys here. We just want to end this."

Red stopped, taking a moment as if to even herself out, and her expression turned calm again.

But Laney had gone still, her gaze empty.

Noah started in alarm, almost already knowing what was going to happen next.

And when Laney started to scream so loud, it startled Verren, making him let her go.

Laney's hands flew up to either side of her head again, her

legs immediately turning to jelly, before she collapsed on the floor, seizing violently.

"Laney!" Noah called out, his voice still hoarse.

The look in Red's eyes was critical at the most as she merely watched Laney have a fit on the floor. "What's going on?"

Noah's expression was urgent. "She's having a 'bleed through'," he snapped. "Untie me! I have to help her."

Red looked mildly puzzled. "What is a *bleed through*?"

"I have to help her! Let me go!"

"I'll get a sedative," Verren said, rushing to a table.

"Verren, did we give her something that could cause this?" Red wanted to know.

"Not me." He shook his head as he prepared a shot in a syringe.

Laney was still crumpled on the floor, shrieking like a banshee, racked in pain, her hands pressed to her head.

"Do something!" Noah demanded, struggling against his bindings so forcefully he was managing to rattle the heavy slab.

"Oh, this is a trick, isn't it?" Red's eyes shone. "It's some kind of diversion."

"For god's sake, let me go!"

Laney was still convulsing, the 'bleed through' having lasted longer than her previous episode in the car. Then after another minute, she stopped moving altogether and fell slack on the floor.

Everything was quiet.

Verren looked over, vile of sedative still in his hand.

Noah's eyes widened. "What happened?" He looked frantically back and forth between Red and Verren. "What happened? Answer me!" He struggled even harder against his bindings, jerking up as though he wanted to tear them all apart with his bare hands. "Laney!" he yelled, but all he could do was look on in distress as Laney stayed still. She didn't respond or stir or breathe. "Laney!"

Red raised an eyebrow as she cautiously stepped up to Laney to nudge her in the side with the toe of her shoe.

Nothing.

Noah looked ashen. "What have you done? Laney! No!"

Verren walked over and bent down to check Laney's vitals. It didn't take him long. He looked up to meet Red's gaze with a slight shrug.

Noah's eyebrows furrowed in protest. "No. No! You're wrong. Check again!" he demanded. "I said check her again!" He was heaving in despair, a lump in his throat.

Verren straightened up, stuffing his hands in his lab coat pockets.

Red eyed Laney's dead body. "Hmm." She wrinkled her nose in distaste. "We should probably get someone to clean that up."

Noah shot the two of them a look of disbelief. "What the hell is wrong with you people? You just—" he broke off, dropping his gaze, his chest constricting as though he'd been torn apart.

Red put her hands up as though she couldn't understand the intensity of his anger. "What?" Then she gestured a wave at Verren, presumably to go get someone to "clean it up." "It's just as well. We couldn't study her anyway," she went on in the most casual of tones.

She watched Verren disappear past the plastic sheet curtain. "And even if we were so inclined, we couldn't figure out where to send her back either." She shrugged. "As far as we could tell, her world doesn't exist."

"Of course her world exists," Noah replied, glaring murderously up at Red.

"Well, we couldn't detect it. Unless..." she trailed off and after a moment, her eyes cleared. "Ohhh..."

"Oh, what?"

"Oh, that is fascinating," Red murmured in awe, her expression glazed in deep thought.

He studied her expression. "Something *was* happening to her homeworld." He narrowed his eyes in conclusion. "And you know what it is."

She waved him away.

"Tell me!" he demanded.

Red rolled her eyes. "Oh, calm down." She regarded him with a plain look. "Ever...snag your arm on a tree branch, running in the woods? Or by the looks of you, your training obstacle course?" she amended.

"What happens next?" she went on to prompt. "You get a little gash, might bleed a little, maybe a lot. But guess what? The human body is a wonderful thing." She tilted her head. "You tell me. You'll know the answer to this, Mr. Genius. What happens to an open wound after a few days, say, maybe even after a few weeks?"

Noah blinked as the answer popped into his head. "It heals..."

Red looked self-satisfied. "Precisely," she said. "Will you believe me when I say that the multiverse likely has the same nature?"

He looked thrown. "What are you saying? You're saying that her homeworld is healing itself? Reforming itself around a configuration wherein Laney no longer exists?"

"Wherein she *never* existed," she enunciated. "And I didn't say 'healing'," she corrected. "I mean she seemed so desperate, it must have been a while ago now. By this point, I'm betting it's healed itself already."

"No."

"How long?"

"Eight months."

She threw up her hands in incredulous disbelief. "Come on! She's been displaced for *eight* months? Even celery grows faster than that." Then she smacked her palm on her forehead at her epiphany. "That's why she was so fuzzy on our scans!" Then she blew out a breath. "Well, I guess it doesn't matter now, does it?"

Noah swallowed hard.

He felt weak.

He closed his eyes.

20

Out of Mind

Laney opened her eyes.

She was lying on the floor.

What the hell just happened?

Her heart began to pound.

Danger.

Her eyes popped wide as she tried to look around without moving but upon seeing nobody else around, she figured she could lift her head to check again.

The lab was empty.

Laney groaned, pushing through the pain to get up. Her head felt like it was split in two, she felt sore all over, and something under her ear was throbbing badly. She felt up her neck.

Her CCL! Her eyes lit up as everything came rushing back to her.

She must have had a 'bleed through.' But how was she still alive?

Then she blinked in the recall. "Oh shit. Noah," she mumbled in alarm, whirling around to see Noah still bound to the heavy slab, unconscious again.

Except for this time, it didn't look like he was breathing.

Oh no. She bit her lip as she rushed over.

She was looking around the lab fervently to figure out how to free him when someone caught her from behind. "Aagh!"

Verren had wound his arm around Laney's neck in a chokehold. "What do you think you're doing?" he hissed. "Did you have a good nap?"

Laney coughed, trying her best to struggle free, her arms flailing on either side. "Ugh," she croaked.

"How are you alive?" he demanded. "What are you?" He squeezed her neck. "Tell me!"

She wailed in pain, racking her brain in distress, but she was no match for him. Then her eyes caught Noah's stuff on the table and she tried to make a break for it, hoping to catch Verren off-guard with her sudden movement.

But he slammed her against the table, his grip around her neck tightening. "You know, if it was up to me, you'd all be dead by now," he relayed with a sneer.

Laney was waving her hand over the table desperately as she choked, scattering objects around, some of them dropping on the floor with a loud clatter.

"The boss thinks you should all be studied, but I think that's giving you too much credit," Verren spoke hoarsely. "You know I lost my whole family in a sinkhole, caused by that damn spacetime disruption. One that swallowed three cities."

Laney cried out loud as she stretched to try to reach for something, her fingertips just brushing against it. *Just a little bit closer...* She squeezed her eyes shut in concentration and only felt her fingers close around a little cylinder.

The next thing Verren knew, Laney had jabbed the memory serum syringe right into his arm.

"Aaahh!" Verren screeched. "What the hell was that?" he asked, seemingly not even hurt at all and still holding on to her.

Laney's eyes were smarting from desperation. She had zero options left. She was close to passing out. She peeked up at Noah still unconscious on the slab. *Noah...* She tried to wheeze in enough air into her lungs, trying to kick and struggle loose from Verren's python-like grip.

Almost at her last breath, Verren's grip loosened and he finally collapsed on the floor.

Laney sprang away, grabbing onto the table for support, gasping and coughing, trying to suck in oxygen until her throat felt raw.

She staggered toward the slab where Noah was, examining some buttons closely until she found the release button and he collapsed off the slab, falling right onto her. "Oh, ow," she groaned as he was too heavy for her to hold upright. She sank to the floor with him.

He still didn't seem to be breathing.

Laney furrowed her eyebrows, shifting to prop his head on her lap, even with her hands shaking. She glanced up furtively to see if Verren's racket had caught anyone else's attention but it seemed they were in luck.

She looked down at Noah, trying to focus so as not to completely freak out. "Noah. Noah?" She patted his cheek lightly at first then harder. "Oh please, please, please." She brushed his hair off his forehead. "Wake up. Please wake up. Please be alive."

She gritted her teeth, looking around again. If Red came back, they would both be done for. "Noah? Come on, do you hear me? We have to go now. Wake up," she urged, stroking his cheek.

Noah didn't wake up, didn't respond, didn't move.

Laney frowned, a wave of annoyance coming over her. "Dammit, Noah," she cursed, her teeth clenched. "I didn't come all this way for nothing. Wake the hell up!"

But he remained still, lifeless, his face pale.

Her breath caught in her throat.

What if Noah was dead?

She would really have to leave him.

Laney's shoulders sank, her entire being felt heavy. She sat with an empty stare, having almost lost the will to move altogether. Her stomach felt like a pit.

It felt different to leave him knowing he would simply be stuck in another world, as opposed to knowing it wouldn't make a difference because he was actually gone.

Noah was gone.

There was a deep stinging ache forming inside her.

It felt like it was cutting right through.

And a part of her was slowly sinking into a deep, dark abyss.

Noah...

Just then, with a deep breath, Noah's eyes opened.

Laney's eyes lit up. "Noah?"

His eyelids were heavy when he met her gaze. "Laney?" he spoke uncertainly, as if in awed reverence.

She felt like laughing out loud. Her smile almost cracked her face, her chest constricting in incredible relief and disbelief, her eyes watering as she cradled his face in her hands. "Hi."

His forehead was creased, his voice quiet. "I thought I lost you."

She sniffed, managing to tone down her smile, not to mention her racing pulse. "I thought I lost *you.*"

He groaned as he tried to sit up. "How did you—are you okay? I thought you...died just now."

Laney shook her head quickly as she helped him to stand up and gather up his stuff. "I have no idea but right now, you have to help me." She hastened toward the quantum jump machine. First things first. "We need to destroy this thing."

"What?" he grunted lightly as he put his jacket back on.

"Come on." She waved him over. "You're the scientist. You need to disable it. Make sure that girl can't open up a quantum shear to invade your world. Do you know how?"

Noah's eyebrows rose. "Do I know how to tamper with what's basically an electromagnetic generator?" His tone was almost mocking.

"*Without* hurting anybody," Laney amended, meeting his gaze pointedly. "This ship has tens of thousands of innocent people on it."

He rolled his eyes, groaning again as he bent down under the mechanism to have a look. "*I'm* hurt, but who cares, right?"

Laney was craning her neck, keeping a lookout. She put her hands on her hips and peered over his shoulder. "You figure it out?"

He grunted in the effort. "Back at GNR, eight months ago, it was the main capacitor that had blown out and I'm betting...aha!" He pulled out a little shelf compartment from under the enclosure. "They use the same approach. The raw material these things use takes decades to regenerate, so all we'll need to do is—"

"STOP!"

Laney whirled around upon hearing Red's voice call out from the doorway. She put her hand up and shot Red a warning look. "Stay back!"

"You don't know what you're doing." Red's tone was low, grave.

"Oh, I think he does." Laney gestured to Noah.

Noah straightened up from underneath the quantum jump machine, eyeing Red warily, even as he held the extracted machine component in his hands.

"You're about to destroy years of hard work," Red pointed out, her eyes wide in urgency.

Laney shot her a mocking look. "Then maybe you should have put your years of hard work to better use. You think we're just going to let your giant invasion army attack Noah's world?"

Red looked at her, almost in astonishment. "That's what you think we're trying to do? You think that's my mission?"

Laney cast Noah a puzzled glance before prompting Red, "If not that, then what?"

Red shook her head in resolve. "There's no way I'm risking opening another hole in the universe. If we let these incursions keep happening, the entire spacetime continuum will unravel. It will destroy us all," she declared.

Laney's jaw almost dropped as it dawned on her. "You're trying to—"

"*I'm* trying to trigger a countering chain reaction to fix *your* mess. And our data suggests it starts with his world. Like I said before, we're not the bad guys here. All we want is to end this. *Everywhere*," Red stated. "Nobody should have this capability. It's for the good of everyone. We need to close the window."

Laney leaned slightly toward Noah. "Can she really do that?"

"I'd imagine the technology required to open a quantum shear is similar to one that can seal it," Noah replied, his eyes narrowed in disdain.

But Red's gaze was pinned on Laney. "Tell me the truth, Miss Carter. You want the interdimensional shears sealed just as much as I do, don't you? You understand the danger it poses. You've seen it first-hand. Heck, it's the reason you're stuck here to begin with."

Laney's mouth dropped open slightly as Red's words hit home.

Noah frowned at Laney's expression. "Laney, don't listen to her," he advised. "Besides, if she closes the window now, you'll be trapped in this dimension. And you know damn well, they'll just keep you in a box for the rest of your life." He glanced at her. "We don't belong here. We need to go home."

Red blinked at him. "Oh." She caught on a slightly quizzical expression. "You haven't told her."

Laney felt another deep pit in her stomach. "Told me what?"

Red gave her a wan look. "Honey, you have nowhere to go. Your homeworld has reset. Just like I told your boyfriend."

Laney turned stunned eyes over to Noah.

He met her gaze, an off-guard hint of guilt in his eyes. "I was going to tell you."

But Laney furrowed her eyebrows, the wheels in her head spinning. What if it was true? If she couldn't go home, then did it really matter anymore where she went? Would it matter anymore what happened to her?

She met Red's steely gaze again before looking up at Noah.

Maybe this was it. Maybe this was the solution. To close all the interdimensional windows. Even if it meant she was trapped here forever.

"Laney?" Noah looked wary.

"What if she's right?" Laney's voice was quiet.

"What do you mean 'what if she's right'?"

She gave him a meaningful look. "This technology. It *is* dangerous. Maybe we do need to seal all the interdimensional windows."

He looked determined. "Laney, I know you want to fix this. First of all, it's not your mess. But second of all, whether she's right or not, sacrificing your life is not the solution to anything." Then he tossed a glance back at Red. "Besides, she could be lying," he accused out loud. "We can't trust her."

Red chuckled in her throat. "You think I care if you believe me?" She moved her hand slowly and before Laney could figure out what she was doing, Red's little silver handgun was already aimed straight at Laney's face. "I've got work to do."

Laney froze.

"Now step away from the machine. Both of you." Red flicked her weapon to gesture them to move.

Noah's eyes were pinned on Red's weapon as he stepped sideways, not wanting to make any sudden movements.

"Put the capacitor down," Red told Noah, training the weapon onto him.

Laney narrowed her eyes. "You're not going to shoot him. You need him to make your machine work."

"Maybe," Red replied deadpan. "But I didn't say I needed him to be able to walk."

Laney put her hands up in an attempt to placate her. "Look, I understand where you're coming from," she began. "Eleanor has royally messed with all of us, but there must be another way."

Red sneered. "You think I've wasted years of my life on this when there's another way? This is our only defense. My world is counting on this for our survival." Her expression faded. "They're counting on *me*," she added, faltering a little and as she spoke, she lowered her weapon a smidge.

The instant that Red was distracted, Noah immediately dove for the gun.

Red yelped in alarm, firing off a shot in a knee-jerk reaction.

Laney jumped in fright, falling back on the floor.

The shot clanked on metal.

Laney opened her eyes and looked down. Noah had tossed the capacitor tray into her hands and Red had shot a hole through it with the bullet intended for Laney.

"NO!" Red yelled in dismay.

Noah knocked the weapon out of Red's hands and he pinned her face down on the ground, twisting her arm behind her even as she tried to kick away, screeching. "You have no idea what you've just done. This is the future. These are the weapons. You can't stop it. You two are making a huge mistake!"

Laney was still heaving. She pushed herself up off the floor as she stared at Red who was struggling like mad to get free, but quick as a flash, Noah moved to knock her out and Red slackened on the floor, unconscious.

Noah looked up and met Laney's somber gaze, a concerned crease on his forehead. "Are you okay?"

She nodded, even as she was still trying to shake off her frazzled nerves. She almost felt sorry for Red. But it wasn't that Laney couldn't sympathize with her mission. It was just that she had her own. They were all each only trying to protect their own worlds.

Laney clenched her jaw with a renewed resolve. "We have to move," she directed, her tone authoritative as she gestured for Noah to follow her.

"Wait." Noah stopped. "Aren't we on some sort of space station? How are we going to get out of here?"

"Yeah." She bit her lip. "I kind of have an idea about that."

He gave her an incredulous look. "You do?"

"Come on." She waved him over as she headed for the door, stopping short and pressing back against the wall as a couple of guards strolled by, chuckling and talking among themselves.

Noah peered around and met her gaze with a nod signaling all clear before they sneaked out the door to head down the corridor.

Laney arrived at a doorway, her gaze wandering around, trying to figure out how to open it.

"What is this place?" Noah assessed the control panel.

Aha. Her eyes lit up as she spotted a button labeled "Manual open" and the moment she pressed it, the door slid open with another loud shush.

Noah's eyes widened.

Beyond the door was the hangar that Laney had walked past earlier.

She met his gaze. "Can you fly a ship?"

He shrugged. "I guess we'll find out." He looked around warily to make sure the coast was clear before they moved out of their hiding spot and ran onto the flight deck, dodging behind ships and equipment until they came up to a spacecraft with its canopy open.

"Get in." Noah motioned Laney up, almost shunting her up into the back seat.

A loud horn blared.

Laney's eyes lit up in alarm as she slid into the deep chair. "Uh-oh."

Noah hopped into the pilot seat, surveying all the buttons and switches on the panel in front of him.

Laney couldn't see him from behind the chair but she tried to crane her neck. "Why aren't we moving yet?"

"Would you give me a minute? I've never flown a...a space-craft before," he retorted.

"Oh boy," Laney mumbled in dread as she saw about a dozen uniformed security staff, charging onto the flight deck, yelling loudly. She heard shots being fired and a couple pinged off the safety glass canopy of the spacecraft.

She ducked in fright. "Holy shit! They're shooting at us!"

"Yeah, I noticed." Noah's tone was dry as he continued to flip switches and buttons until finally, the spacecraft began to move.

"Let's go! Let's go!" she hollered, hammering on the back of Noah's seat.

Noah got the spacecraft to speed up and it rumbled down the deck headed toward the open port—just as the exterior doors began to close.

"*Come on!*" Noah yelled out in frustration.

Laney was already wincing, bracing her hands against the back of Noah's seat.

She ducked again with a startled scream as she heard the spacecraft take on more weapons fire even as it sped faster, almost ramming the closing exterior doors, rattling it to just barely scrape past.

Noah blew out a breath.

"We made it!" Laney whooped.

The spacecraft had gathered enough momentum to get propelled clear of The Aquila's orbit but they still needed to go faster to escape.

"I'm trying to find the thrusters," Noah was saying.

But Laney was already staring at the cracks forming on

the safety glass canopy of the spacecraft caused by the bullet holes. "Noah," she called out. "The glass is going to break."

Noah cursed out loud and began rummaging around the pilot seat. "They must have respirators here or something."

"Oh, no, no, no, no—" Laney edged back in her seat.

Then something materialized in empty space above them.

"Oh my god, it's the Dauntless!" Laney exclaimed in sheer joy.

"The what?"

Laney watched in anticipation as the docking bay door beneath the hull of the Dauntless opened up as though to scoop them out of the void but then she frowned as she spotted an even larger crack forming on the spacecraft canopy.

The Dauntless was still over a hundred yards away.

She wailed. "Oh no, no, we're not gonna make it."

"Ohhh *shit*." Noah's voice sounded incredibly annoyed.

Laney turned and glimpsed another squad of spacecraft launching from The Aquila in pursuit.

The ships were already shooting at them. Not that they weren't deep enough in trouble. The giant crack on their spacecraft canopy had come into its own.

She closed her eyes momentarily as the glass exploded, leaving shattered pieces of it floating about in space.

She wanted to scream, if only she didn't have to exhale all the air out of her lungs before the vacuum suffocated her— just as their ship skidded and scraped into the Dauntless' docking bay, very nearly smashing against the interior wall, right as the doors closed with a loud pressurizing shush.

And Trin's voice came loud and clear on the PA.

"Welcome back, guys. Brace yourselves."

Laney met Noah's astonished gaze as she gasped a big deep breath in, grinning wide in indescribable relief.

"Space jump in 3, 2, 1..."

21

Safe Space

Laney stepped out of her quarters after getting cleaned up. It felt like she had washed the last few days of chaos off of her.

And the relative silence of space was providing a stillness that for once, she wasn't feeling an impending sense of doom.

Sigrid had reported that they were on approach to Betelgeuse and that the supernova had miraculously not yet occurred.

Laney had never been so glad to be on time in her entire life.

She was walking down the corridor on the upper deck heading to the bridge when she heard heavy thuds coming from behind her. She turned and saw Sol coming around the corner.

She gave Laney a big smile. "Laney! So glad you made it back."

"Hi, Sol," she greeted. "Heading to the bridge?"

Sol nodded, holding up a little tablet. "I've got a report on all essential systems. It's almost 'go' time. This is the first supernova we're going to be observing this close," she relayed. "Not to mention, we gotta be quick to haul ass if we don't want to get our tails severely singed," she added with a wink as they arrived at the bridge.

The two of them paused by the doorway. Laney felt a smile of wonder as she sighted the very bright star in clear view on the main window against the black vastness of space.

The red supergiant Betelgeuse was about to put on a show.

It was going to be spectacular.

She glanced over and spotted Trin, Dek, and Noah, looking to be having an important discussion around Dek's console station.

It looked like Noah had also cleaned up and changed, except he had left his jacket off.

Laney's stomach fluttered at the mere sight of him. Mostly in relief.

She could barely believe that they had managed to rescue him, escape from the generation ship, and foil the plans of The Alliance.

Her smile widened.

Everything was going to be okay now.

"So, that's him, huh?" Sol elbowed her then whistled. "Now I get why you were so eager to rescue him. I would be too if my primary looked like that," she remarked as she walked past her.

Laney made a face, flushing a little. "It's not—that's not—," she hissed then stopped short, merely rolling her eyes as she followed Sol toward Cam's workstation. "Hey, Cam."

Cam looked up at them with narrowed eyes. "What are you girls gossiping about?"

"Primaries," Sol piped up.

Laney hurried to cut in before Sol could go on. "The Commander and Dek," she supplied, making Sol chuckle to herself. "They seem well-matched," she observed.

"Oh yeah," Cam informed her. "They make a fantastic team. Dek is a really good grounding influence on the Commander, and she opens doors for him that he otherwise wouldn't."

"Huh." Laney nodded, looking fascinated. "Have you ever seen them fight?" she asked in a hushed voice so that only Cam and Sol could hear.

Cam was already nodding.

"Oh, sure," Sol confirmed. "Being primaries doesn't mean you get along twenty-four seven. People are still people after all."

Laney smirked. *Sounds about right.* It still felt odd to acknowledge that Noah might be her primary. They hadn't even had a chance to talk yet since coming back from The Aquila.

Hold that thought.

She felt a warmth in her stomach, remembering Noah's words back at GNR.

"Laney!"

Laney looked up, snapping to attention, and saw Trin beckoning her over to the big chair. She walked up, giving Dek a nod in greeting as she passed him, before looking up at Noah, but he appeared focused on some screens on a wall panel.

"Listen," Trin started to Laney. "I'm sorry about throwing you in the escape pod before. I figured the easiest way for you to find Dr. Donovan in that giant spaceship would be to get captured yourself."

Laney gave her a look. "How did you even know we'd be able to escape?"

Trin pursed her lips, meeting her gaze evenly. "How did you know we'd come back for you?"

Laney laughed. "Fair point. Though next time, you could warn a girl." She beamed, grateful. "But thanks. Thank you so much."

Trin gestured to Noah. "I've had the rundown of what happened on the generation ship from Dr. Donovan's report." Her expression sobered a little. "So I understand it was the other Laney who caused the spacetime distortion on our world."

Laney made a face. "I'm so sorry."

Trin gave her a small, reassuring smile. "You don't have to be sorry." She gestured to her big chair. "As you can see, from where I'm sitting, the universe looks pretty sweet."

"What's going to happen to The Dauntless now?" Laney knit her eyebrows in concern. "I'm sure The Aquila will have seen you helping us escape. I mean, what other ship in the fleet has space-folding capabilities?"

"With all due respect, they will have to catch us first, Miss Carter."

Laney jumped in surprise and had to laugh.

"Sigrid, we're having a private conversation," Trin reprimanded, sounding more exasperated than displeased.

"Sorry, Commander."

Dek, Sol, and Cam were all sharing a chuckle, having heard Sigrid's assertive declaration on the PA, and Trin was shaking her head, but Laney could tell that everyone on The

Dauntless appreciated Sigrid's unique personality as though she was simply any other member of the crew.

"She's not wrong though," Trin spoke up. "And I'm sure The Alliance has enough problems at the moment. From what I understand, that machine you sabotaged will set them back a couple of years at least."

"But they'll just build it again, won't they?" Laney guessed with not even a shadow of doubt in her tone.

Trin put her hand on Laney's shoulder, tilting her head, self-assuredly. "Then when the time comes, we'll just have to be ready, won't we?"

"Okay, Commander. I have him back," Dek announced, pressing some buttons on his console.

"Hello?" Berry's voice crackled over the PA again.

"Greetings, Dr. Vermillion."

"Hey Sigrid," he responded. "How's it going?"

Noah's eyebrows furrowed in surprise and puzzlement as he looked up. "Is that Berry?"

"Just peachy. I have new blast shielding installed for the supernova."

"That sounds amazing. I can't wait to hear about the neutrino flux readings from a type two supernova. It's going to be magnificent."

Dek leaned over to Trin and Laney with a grin. "Perhaps they'd like to be left alone," he joked under his breath.

Trin cleared her throat loudly, pointedly.

"Oh. Sorry." Berry stopped short to refocus. "Hey. Dek. Trin. Guys. Did you find Laney?"

"Yes, Berry. She's right here. And so is Dr. Donovan."

"WHAT?"

"We—Well…we've just mounted a rescue for your other friend from the Alliance ship."

"You did *what*?" Berry's disbelief was not disguised.

"Hey, it was Laney's idea," Dek pointed out.

Laney's cheeks reddened. "I mean, well, you said to not get separated."

Berry's chuckle resounded over the PA.

"Berry." Noah approached Dek's station. "You could have told us you had a way to communicate with this world."

"Oh. Well, we had very limited information about that world in the preliminary studies and there was a lot of inter-ference the first time around. I wasn't sure it was even going to work again and I didn't want to get your hopes up."

"Sure. Wouldn't want us to be too hopeful," Laney scoffed, her tone wry.

Dek laughed.

"Listen, Berry," Noah began. "There's a chance that the boomerang path may be invalid. One of the worlds we jumped through to get here may have been…sucked into a singularity."

"Oh shoot," Laney piped up with a grimace. "Speaking of bad news, Berry, I just remembered, I'm also going to need another dose of that memory serum."

"What? Why?" Noah was the one to ask.

"I had to dose Verren with it to get away."

"You what?" He gave her a look of disbelief.

Laney shrugged pointedly. "Well it worked, didn't it?"

Berry chuckled again. "What in the name of Sam Hill have you two been up to since you left here?"

Laney shook her head. "Dude, you seriously don't want to know."

"Well then, I actually have good news," Berry announced. "Trin and Dek sent me the information about Eleanor's appearance on that world two years ago and I found the path she used to get there."

Laney's eyes lit up. "You did?"

"When I was digging through Eleanor's old transcripts," Berry went on. "I kept finding a strange footnote, but without this context, it was meaningless. Basically, Eleanor found maybe a one in a quadrillion traversal path probability—a shortcut, if you will. Except she did it all by herself, without the help of any search algorithm. I'm transmitting the configuration to you now so you can program it on the Zeta device."

"That's awesome, Berry!" Laney was more than elated.

Eleanor really *was* the gift that kept on giving. She was like the biggest villain and the biggest hero. The only one who could get them into this much trouble, but also the only one who could get them out.

"Fifteen minutes and thirty-five seconds to the solar core collapse, Commander."

Berry sort of squeaked on the PA. "This is so exciting! I can't believe you guys are about to witness a red supergiant supernova up close."

"Cam, move us to within fifty-million kilometers of the star," Trin called out.

"Aye."

Dek looked over at Laney. "Laney, you'll need to remove anything metal on you."

Laney's eyes lit up. "Oh, yes, please." Her hand flew up to the gadget under her ear. She couldn't wait to take the aching thing off. "Berry, how do I get this flipping CCL off?"

"Noah will have to detach it safely." Berry's voice crackled a little over the radio. "Do you have a laser micro-scalpel?"

Dek gestured to a lab adjacent to the bridge. "You can use the lab in the back," he said. "Sigrid, why don't you transfer Dr. Vermillion's signal into Lab 1?"

"Certainly."

"Right." Laney nodded, glancing up at Noah who had already gone ahead.

"Can you believe this? I'm about to get barbecued in a supernova," Laney announced in mocking as she entered the doorway labeled "Lab 01" with the door shushing closed behind her.

Berry's voice came over the comms system. "Don't worry, Laney. The hyper-intense shock exposure from the supernova should simply neutralize the levels of dark energy you were exposed to with Eleanor's interdimensional insulation."

Laney shrugged. "I don't know why I'm not even nervous. Then again, given my week, I'm seriously hoping there's nowhere else to go but up."

Berry chuckled again.

She spotted Noah's jacket draped over the table inside the lab, as well as a few of his things scattered on the table. "What were you doing in here?" she asked him.

"I was trying to fix my HUD before. But I couldn't. I'd have to get back to my world first," Noah explained, his tone serious as usual as he shifted things on the table to make space.

At that, Laney's expression turned melancholy. "Hey," she began. "About what that girl on The Aquila said about my world. Is it possible? Could it be gone?"

Noah's expression blanked for a moment. "Maybe." He shrugged. "I admit I already had a similar theory, that your world might be undergoing some type of flux as a result of your displacement. But I didn't figure it could be happening so fast."

Laney took a moment to process the information as that might finally explain why Kevin was doing all that stuff with Darla. They didn't betray her. They had simply forgotten all about her. She made a face as neither was a desirable outcome.

"But it didn't look like it was finished. It was still fluxing when we were there," he went on with a dismissive tone. "There's still hope. You can still make it. We should stick to the mission."

"Dek sent me Noah's report." Berry had a bit of remorse in his tone. "I'm so sorry about what happened on The Aquila with your CCL. I mean, I *did* program a failsafe trigger on it," he informed them. "But I never envisioned that it would affect the wearer, much more that it would also shut down your vitals along with it."

"Don't worry about it," Laney dismissed. "The way I figure, that failsafe probably saved my life."

"That's great. Isn't that great, Noah?" Berry prompted.

Noah cleared his throat, looking uncomfortable. "Sure."

"Either way, I'd like to have my brain all to myself again, so if you please?" she quipped as she walked toward him.

Noah stiffened as she got closer.

Laney knit her eyebrows as she noticed. She'd been getting some strange standoffish vibes from him, not unlike how he was when they had first met. He hadn't even looked at her yet since she'd come in.

"Noah, is everything okay?"

"It's fine." He busied himself prepping the tools on the table.

Laney watched him with a wary, knowing look. "Look, I can tell when something's bothering you too, you know?"

Noah paused, still not meeting her gaze, and when he spoke, his tone was grim. "Dek told me you were already half-way to Betelgeuse when you came back for me."

Laney nodded. "Sure."

His gaze finally snapped to hers, his eyes sharp. "I can't believe you did that."

She blinked, taken aback. "What?"

"You took an incredible risk, Laney," Noah told her off.

She gave him a deadpan look. "Uh, yeah. To save your life."

He grunted in reply, looking away again.

She looked confused. "Are you mad at me?"

He shook his head. It was obvious he was trying hard to keep his cool. "Just—don't do that again."

"What, save your life? You save my life all the time."

"That's different."

She folded her arms across her chest, giving him an expectant look. "How?"

"I don't know!" He threw up his hands in frustration, turning his back to her.

"A-hem!" Berry cleared his throat loudly as though to remind them that he could still hear everything.

Laney winced.

Noah let out a sigh and walked up to the communications panel on the wall. "We'll contact you again later, Berry."

"Okay, but—" Berry's statement cut off as Noah flicked the switch.

22

Inevitable

"What's going on, Noah?"

He pursed his lips for a moment before answering, his voice low. "I want to apologize."

"Apologize?" Laney echoed, mystified.

He cracked his neck in unease. "Back at GNR," he began. "I shouldn't have said all that stuff. And I had absolutely no right to ask what I did."

"What?" She furrowed her eyebrows in confusion, displeasure, annoyance. "Are you—taking it back?"

Noah glanced over. "When I thought you'd died back on The Aquila..." he began, sounding pained. "That was the worst thing I'd ever thought I could experience. And I should have realized this sooner." He averted his gaze. "You're not safe with me. You were right before. We don't belong together. You have to go home. Be with Kevin."

Laney scoffed, looking away, almost in exasperated

disbelief. "Oh my god. It's Casablanca." She threw up her hands. "I'm in Casablanca right now."

His entire posture had sagged. "I can't protect you. I've almost lost you so many times. It's not good enough. I'm not good enough."

She peered up at him. "I don't care about that. And I can take care of myself. I'm not afraid anymore." She shook her head. "I can't leave you again. I already knew it. From the car crash. Halfway to Betelgeuse."

"You're only saying that because of the theory. You don't even believe the theory."

"It doesn't matter," Laney stated almost carelessly. "Theory or no theory, I'm choosing you."

He wavered, a heavy meaningful look in his eyes. "Are you ready for that? Like really ready? You would have to give up everything. Your family, your friends. Your whole world. Are you ready to give all that up? You have a chance," he implored. "You could have a normal life. I want you to have it."

"I don't want to have a normal life if you're not in it," she avowed. "So if you're asking if I'm ready to exchange all that, then my answer is: yes, I'm ready."

"No, you're not."

"Yes, I am."

"No, you're not."

"Yes, I—"

"Well, I'm not!" he cut in. "I'm *not* ready for you to give all that up." He blew out a breath in weariness. "You said it yourself. In your world, you don't have to worry about these kinds of things, worlds collapsing, multiple dimensions. That's what

I want for you. I want you to be safe. And on your world, you will be."

Laney felt a constriction in her chest. "No, but—"

Noah shook his head, reaching up to tuck her hair behind one ear. "Let me do this," he pled with a small smile. "I've been selfish right from the start. Eleanor stole your life. I want to give it back."

Laney's heart went thud in her stomach. His logic was undeniable, but it still stung like hell. She looked up into his eyes and recognized his unshakable resolve.

Her own eyes were threatening to well up. She took a deep breath to get a grip before managing a compliant nod, and she happened to cast a glance down at the device on her wrist.

The revolutionary gadget that started it all. Somehow in all the chaos, she hadn't even noticed that it had started working properly again, as it was probably just the time loop at GNR that had made it go haywire.

She frowned, picking at the strap since she'd have to take it off too, but she couldn't seem to figure out how to open the latch. "How do you even take this thing off?"

Noah's voice was soft as he explained. "It's DNA-activated. You'll have to swipe it to unlock."

She undid the latch and detached the Zeta device from her wrist. "Here." She took his hand to place the device in his palm. "I guess my mission is over." She looked up and met his intense gaze again.

"Thank you," Noah said after a moment, his tone solemn. "For coming to save me. I always knew you had it in you."

She bit her lip, stifling her hopeless chuckle. "Well, you know, you can never keep yourself out of trouble without me."

At that, he swallowed hard, his forehead creasing as he reached out for her, pulling her against him. She nestled her face in the hollow of his neck, squeezing her eyes shut, not willing to move an inch otherwise, and she felt him tighten his arms around her.

"Laney," he murmured against her hair and she realized his heartbeat was also pounding in his chest.

She shook her head again. She already knew what he was going to say.

"Don't worry. Everything will be okay. You'll get your cure. I'll take you back to your world. And it will be just like none of this ever happened."

Her chest constricted again at the finality of his words. "I can't believe this is happening. Why did this have to happen at all?"

"Look at me."

It took some effort to lift her face, but as soon as she looked into his deep blue eyes, she felt a warm rush all over.

A corner of his mouth turned up, as though the same thing had just happened to him. But there was sadness in his eyes, the sadness of truth, of inevitability.

He drew a shaky breath in, leaning his face closer, his forehead almost touching hers, before speaking his declaration softly, fervently.

"I am yours."

And Laney's vision blurred with tears.

"In any world. In any multiverse," he went on, heaving himself. His gaze dropped to her mouth and Laney noticed him clench his jaw, as though to try to keep his control.

Her lips parted as if to say something, but as soon as

Noah felt her breath against his, he took her lips in his in a dizzying, all-consuming kiss.

Sigrid pretended to clear her throat.

Laney broke off and met Noah's gaze again.

"Miss Carter. Dr. Donovan. Sorry to interrupt. The solar output is peaking."

Noah straightened up, his forehead creasing in suspicion. "Was she listening the whole time?"

Laney's shoulders shook in slight mirth. "I don't even want to ask," she said with a sigh. "Well. Before we forget," she noted in reminder, tilting her head to one side so they could get back to their original business of detaching her CCL.

Noah signaled a nonchalant shrug, picking up the laser micro-scalpel before carefully disengaging Laney's CCL. After a few minutes, the gadget let out a long, low beep in deactivation and then dropped into Noah's palm.

Laney's face paled instantly.

Noah looked alarmed. "What?"

She put her arms around herself. "It's so c-cold," she stammered, shivering.

He called out, "Sigrid, what's going on?"

"Miss Carter's internal body temperature has dropped seven degrees."

Noah could see the puffs of air from her breath. "Why?" he pressed.

"Unknown."

Noah rapped on the door and it slid open. "Dek, something's wrong," he alerted. "Laney's body temp just dropped seven degrees."

Dek glanced over, rubbing his chin in thought. "Might

be time for that supernova bath. Come on." He gestured for them to follow him.

Noah scooped Laney up and followed suit after Dek down the narrow corridor to enter another dark doorway.

"What's happening, Noah?" Laney was trembling all over. She felt drowsy, like she was about to black out.

Noah shushed her. "It's going to be okay, Laney. I've got you."

"Noah, bring her here." Dek waved them over and a spotlight shone a bright circle where he stood just before a round platform with a railing around it raised from the floor.

Laney moaned slightly, squinting in the bright light, but she felt too weak to move.

"Laney, this is the viewing turret," Dek explained as Noah placed Laney down onto the platform. "We use it to study stellar phenomena. It'll lift you outside the ship. Normally, we enable all the space shielding on it, but for now, we'll just enable the vacuum seal to make sure you don't suffocate. You need the supernova energy wave to penetrate one-hundred percent."

"Can you hold on?" Noah peered into her face.

"I'll t-try," Laney stuttered as she half-collapsed against the railing.

"All hands. Brace for impact." Trin's voice came over the PA.

Noah stepped back as the protective shielding slid down around the platform.

Dek hurried toward a control console. "We have to time

this exactly," he said then called out. "Sigrid, what's the count?"

"Solar core collapse in 6...5..."

Dek pushed a button on his console and Noah watched the bright light from the viewing turret rise. A port opened up on the roof of the deck and the platform with Laney on it slid upward and out of the ship.

"4...3..."

Noah's anxiety levels cranked up unusually high the moment he couldn't see what was going on with Laney outside the ship.

"2...1..."

Noah braced himself against the wall.

"Core collapse in progress."

The ship shook with the initial energy wave that washed over The Dauntless. From the tiny window in the lab, they could see a blinding light fill the blackness of space for a split second.

Dek was watching a monitor intently. "There, that should do it." He pushed another button and the viewing turret retracted back down with a pneumatic hum.

Laney seemed to be standing upright with her back to them, but as soon as the turret reached the floor level, she collapsed in a heap on the floor.

Noah's eyes widened as he rushed toward her. "Laney!" He hammered on the turret's protective shielding that was still closed. "Open it up!" he called out to Dek before looking back over at Laney. "Laney!" He bent down to try to peer at her face.

She was unconscious. Out of reach.

"Laney!" He was starting to heave. "Is she okay? Dek—is she okay?" he demanded.

"Hold on, Noah," Dek replied calmly as he worked on his control panel. "We need to make sure she's decontaminated from any harmful radiation before we can retract the shielding."

"Laney," Noah said softly, not taking his eyes off her.

A console machine beeped twice and Dek nodded in acknowledgment. He pressed another button and looked up as the shielding retracted with a whoosh.

Noah scooped Laney up in his arms to prop her head on his chest. "Laney?" He shook her shoulder and was somewhat put to ease when he could feel her faintly breathing.

Laney's eyes fluttered open.

"Laney." There was no mistaking the relief in Noah's voice. "You're okay. It's okay."

Laney moaned, making a face. She cleared her throat, before she looked up, blinking, to meet Noah's gaze. "Well..." she started, barely above a whisper.

Noah raised his eyebrows, watching her face, waiting to see what she wanted to say.

"There's something I never thought I could check off my bucket list."

And Noah's chuckle rumbled in his chest, even as he moved to pull her closer against him.

Dek came over and knelt beside them.

"How are you feeling?" Dek asked as he ran some checks

on Laney and clipped something on her thumb that took a small blood sample.

Laney swallowed. "I... Normal."

Dek pressed a few buttons on his tablet gadget. "As far as I can tell, you're perfectly fine. Your O2 stats are normal. You're not getting any surges to your core temperature like you're going to explode in the next thirty seconds. You're all good."

"And the tracking solution?"

After a moment, Dek shook his head. "Not even a trace. You're all clear."

Laney half-smiled, half-moaned in relief as Noah helped her straighten up.

"Dek, how did she go?"

Dek looked up and tapped on his ear communicator. "All good, Commander. It worked." He grinned, standing up himself. "Tell Sol to fire up the K-drive and set a course to about a hundred light-years away from Betelgeuse. That should be safe enough."

"Aye."

The next moment, Laney grabbed Noah's arm, teetering off-balance as the entire ship trembled.

Noah looked around warily. "Was that supposed to happen?"

Dek looked worried. "Sigrid, was the blast shielding damaged in the leading edge of the supernova?"

"Blast shielding at twenty-two percent. Regeneration nominal."

"Then what's going on?" Dek's forehead was creased.

Sol's voice came on the PA.

"Uh, guys, I'm still checking, but for some reason, the K-drive won't come online."

Dek whirled around to rush out the door without a word, concern written all over his face.

Noah took Laney's arm to support her as they followed Dek back to the bridge.

Trin swiveled around in her chair upon hearing the three of them come through the doorway.

"What's happening?" Dek headed straight for his console.

"Something's disrupting the K-drive."

"Something?" Noah raised an eyebrow.

Cam looked hesitant as he analyzed the readings on his console. "Um, I have a theory, but it's not good." He glanced at everyone's expectant looks before he went on. "I hate to suggest this but there's a good chance Laney's exposure to the supernova is causing interference with the ion reactor. And if we can't engage the K-drive, we can't go anywhere beyond sub-light speed."

Laney swallowed in alarm, even as she was still a bit weakened. "If you guys don't get the K-drive back online before the brunt of the solar wave hits, you'll all be toast." She shook her head in resolve. "Noah, we have to get out of here right now."

"Agreed." Noah rushed to grab his jacket from the lab to put it back on.

"Didn't want to rush you out but I guess this is goodbye." Trin gave Laney a short nod from her big chair.

"I can't even begin to thank you," Laney began.

Dek grinned at Laney. "Hey, maybe we'll see you again, you never know." He winked as he moved to strap himself into his chair to get ready for zero-G.

"Not sure if that's a good thing. But I'll be sure to tell Berry to send my regards." She mocked a salute.

Noah raised his hand, giving Trin and Dek an acknowledging nod in return. "Thank you," he bade before ushering Laney out of the bridge.

"This way." Laney led the way down the corridor toward the cargo bay where the quantum shear exit trace was.

Once they were in position, Noah turned to Laney. "Good to go?" he prompted, his eyebrows raised.

Laney took a deep breath.

It was the first time that she was going to make a quantum jump without Eleanor's interdimensional insulation. She wasn't sure what to expect.

23

Going Home

Laney felt as though she had been spewed out of the quantum shear.

She tumbled on the floor, rolling to one side. "Holy—OW!" she groaned out a curse, squeezing her stinging eyes shut as she curled up, coughing.

Then she heard a familiar chuckle.

"Welcome back."

Laney was still grimacing as she looked up to meet Maia's sunny gaze.

Behind Maia, she could see the wavy sparkles of blue light reflected against the interior of the large metal capsule of Berry's submarine that Laney thought she'd never see again.

She almost sighed in relief.

But first, she cast a glance to her side where Noah was collapsed on his knees, recovering himself.

"Jeez, Noah!" she exclaimed her complaint. "How the hell

have you done that so many times?" she gasped, still trying to catch her breath. She didn't want to move at all. "I feel like I've been thrashed, skinned, burned alive, and squashed all at the same time."

Berry chuckled next. "*Aaand* welcome to the club." He moved to the control panel to push some more buttons.

Noah cleared his throat. "Why couldn't it have been that easy?"

"You call that easy?" Laney's face was in stark disbelief.

"It could have been!" Berry insisted. "If we'd had time to wait for the first traversal path to complete, it would have been a cakewalk. But the way I see it, you had luck on your side. As you've already seen, some worlds do tend to change unexpectedly."

"Where are we now?" Noah straightened up to look over Berry's shoulder at the navigation console.

"We're on the way back to Wellington now," Berry replied, referring to a little radar map. "We'd been waiting at a way-point off the coast of Northland."

Laney let Maia help her up and she put her arms around her. "I'm so glad to see you. Did you have any trouble with The Alliance?"

Maia shook her head. "Fortunately, the University got away with only minor damages. The attacks were mostly concentrated in the docks and the government buildings. Your typical sort of anarchy."

Laney threw up her hands. "Oh, that's just great. I broke your world even more. Maia, I just broke your freaking world."

"Look, Laney," Maia began. "You didn't cause any of this.

Whatever unrest happened, the problems have always been there, hiding in plain sight, bubbling beneath the surface trying to get out before you even arrived."

"Yeah, but I was the catalyst." She pressed her hands to her face in frustration. "Your President warned me about this. I guess I've done exactly what they were afraid I'd do."

"From what I've heard, The Alliance is calling for more transparency in the government, more specifically in terms of potentially world-altering GNR programs—the good *and* the bad," she relayed. "They've gathered a lot of support. If you ask me, maybe The Community finally wants to live in the real world." She braced her hands on Laney's shoulders and nodded. "This is a positive change."

Laney shot her a grateful look, unable to help a chuckle. "Of course *you* would think so."

"I'm sorry to interrupt," Berry cut in with a sheepish look. "But we're going to have to do this right away. Before anything else happens," he added meaningfully.

Laney nodded in understanding.

"One more jump to go." Berry paused, giving her a ceremonious look. "The last one."

Laney's heart was pounding in her chest in anticipation. She turned to give Maia another hug. "Thanks. For all your help."

"I'm just glad I can say a proper goodbye this time," Maia told her.

"Here." Berry handed Noah a fresh new memory serum syringe.

Laney eyed the syringe, pursing her lips almost in reluctance. She looked away as Noah put it in his pocket and she took a moment to look around the steel and brass compartment of the submarine, and then at each of her friends as though hoping to brand their memories in her brain, even as she knew they were about to be wiped. Because she also knew, deep down, even if she forgot absolutely everything, she would never be the same again.

Berry met her gaze and gave her a mock salute. "It was a pleasure serving with you, Miss Carter."

"Thanks, Berry." She smiled at him. "You're brilliant. Don't let anybody tell you otherwise."

Noah was already waiting on the platform when Laney stepped back onto it. He leaned toward her the slightest fraction of an inch to vow under his breath.

"Not one minute."

She beamed, her chest feeling full, and when she looked up at him, the expression in his eyes mirrored her own. She averted her gaze after a beat then she wrinkled her nose in consideration. "You know, 'relativity' is a stupid code word."

Noah rolled his eyes, exasperated. "Then you should have come up with one, if you're such a genius."

Berry was chuckling again as he gave the big red button a firm whack with his fist.

The swirling vortex of doom crackled as Laney and Noah stepped through it, just before it dissipated, leaving no trace, as if nothing was ever there at all.

Berry straightened up, clapping the proverbial dust off his hands as he stepped back from the console. "Those two," he remarked with an amused shake of his head.

Maia smirked before musing up to Berry, "Do you think yours will feel like that?"

"What?"

"Your primary."

He shrugged after a moment. "I hope so. Maybe with a little less antagonism."

Maia laughed. "Not me. I hope mine is *exactly* like that. With the fighting and the antagonism. How do you know it's real otherwise?" she quipped.

Berry laughed.

After another two minutes, everything in the lab turned a reddish hue as a quantum shear formed again for Noah's return.

Berry watched expectantly, but his jaw dropped when he saw who actually emerged from the shear.

Maia's eyes nearly popped out. "Laney? What the hell?"

Noah stepped off the platform.

With Laney. Again.

She fell to her knees on the platform, coughing.

"What happened?" Berry looked bewildered, eagerly waiting for answers, even as he watched Noah recover for a minute first.

Noah tried to catch his breath. "It didn't work."

"No kidding." Berry rushed to his toolbox to grab some things.

"The memory serum," Noah relayed. "It didn't work like last time. I gave her the shot but she could still remember everything."

"It didn't work?" Maia pressed, turning to Laney in

incredulous disbelief. "What the hell, Laney? Does nothing normal work on you?"

Laney glared up at her, sounding highly annoyed. "I didn't do anything. It's not my fault!"

"I don't understand how you even got her back through the shear again," Berry said as he approached Laney to take some new readings. "It's a miracle she's not dead."

"Well, I wasn't about to leave her there like that." Noah's tone was sharp.

Maia's eyes were wide with concern. "Also let's not try that again, just in case?" she suggested pointedly.

Berry was frowning over his tools, shaking his head. "She must have built an immunity to the memory serum," he posited. "We won't be able to give her another memory wipe." He shook his head, meeting Laney's gaze. "When The Alliance tried to fix you in that machine last week, it must have affected your ability to absorb these specific proteins. Or your exposure to the supernova has somehow altered your absorption rate."

"Oh, that is just *great!*"

"Can you make a new serum?" Noah looked up at Maia.

Maia's lips were curled in uncertainty. "I'd have to work from scratch to reformulate a new one. It took me years to synthesize the first one."

"Years?" Laney echoed with a desolate groan. "Ugh, I need some air," she mumbled, straightening up.

Berry's eyes lit up. He clicked on his walkie-talkie. "Sammo, surface!"

***

Noah climbed out of the hatch to see Laney standing by the railing on the exterior platform, looking out toward the city.

The submarine had come to the surface halfway into the Wellington harbor, except the city looked barely recognizable.

There were no airships in the sky. Part of the old-fashioned brick building of the airship terminal had crumbled. Several buildings along the waterfront were either collapsed altogether or had visible signs of significant fire damage. There were still traces of black smoke wafting up from what looked like several pockets throughout town from the unrest that had taken place.

It was a pretty gloomy sight at first light.

Noah stood beside Laney, silently, if only to share in the grim view.

The hatch opened again and Berry popped out. "Maia says she'll get to work on the serum as soon as she gets back to her lab," he announced. "But in the meantime, she's making celebratory waffles. I think she's pretty happy you're staying," he added with a wry tone.

Laney scoffed, only slightly amused. *Staying?* She looked out at the devastation in a bit of disbelief. Even with the threats of the interdimensional windows closing, her home-world resetting, and all the confusion about Noah, it had to be the memory serum that inevitably threw a spanner in the works.

Berry walked over to stand at Laney's other side and he leaned forward, his expression guarded. "Are you okay?"

"I don't know. Am I?" she quipped.

Berry shrugged. "Well...the tracking solution is gone," he reminded her. "The Bleed is over. You're free."

"But I'm still stuck here."

He made a face. "Don't think of it as being stuck. Think of it as a...prolonged hiatus," he suggested.

"Prolonged hiatus," she repeated in mocking. She knew that if there was even a small chance her homeworld hadn't reset yet, the odds were that it certainly will have by the time Maia got a new serum developed. It was likely this would indeed be a very prolonged hiatus. Then again, Berry did say that she could survive in a world as long as there was no threat from one organization in particular.

"What about The Alliance? They've finally come out of hiding," Laney mentioned.

"Which is a good thing," Berry pointed out, his eyebrows raised. "Now we can deal with them properly and the odds are they won't be so cavalier as to attempt to abduct you again. If you ask me, they've just given up a huge advantage. Either that or they're finally being civilized."

Laney sighed heavily. *Maybe...* "But they've ruined everything. Look at your beautiful city." She gestured toward the ravaged cityscape.

"Cities can be rebuilt." Noah's tone was somber as always.

Berry nodded in agreement. "And don't forget we're still waiting on that earthquake that could level the city altogether. It's supposed to be a big one," he said with a catch in his tone.

Laney shook her head in mirth. She knew Berry was trying to make her feel better but at the moment, everything felt bittersweet.

"Don't worry, Laney," Berry reassured with a brief pat on her shoulder. "We're all here for you. We'll figure something out."

Laney managed a small smirk. "So?" She threw up her hands. "What the hell am I supposed to do now?"

Berry and Noah exchanged looks: Berry's concerned. Noah's pensive.

Berry shrugged again, at a complete loss. "Shoot if I know. Whatever, I guess." He peered at her face again. "Want to learn some Physics? I could use an assistant."

Laney stifled a desperate incredulous laugh. Somehow she was feeling an odd sense of calm. And at least it was a comfort to know that her family and friends would be fine. They would all likely just adapt to the new world.

And so would she.

She even knew for an absolute fact there were worlds she could be stuck in that were far worse.

She blew out a huge resigned breath even as she was still frowning in deep thought at what the future might bring.

She glanced up to look at Noah.

Noah was looking as intense as ever. He dropped his eyes briefly before meeting her gaze again.

Laney felt Noah take her hand in his.

"Ready?"

And she smiled.

****

The End.

Do you want some EXCLUSIVE **Selfless series** bonus content?

Join S. Breaker's **Sci-fi Readers Facebook community** now!

DON'T MISS AN EPIC ENDING!

S. BREAKER lives in New Zealand with her husband and two kids. She writes non-stop action adventure, offbeat science fiction and fantasy books.

Suburban mum by day and author by night, she loves to live vicariously through her characters. They don't have to vacuum all day long and are almost always guaranteed to survive any fantastical or thrilling incidents, no matter how treacherous she writes them.

She likes binge-watching TV shows and reading books that take her to far enough unknown worlds—but then still have enough time to wash the dishes after.

Subscribe to her mailing list now for bookish news and get a FREE e-book!

https://subscribe.breakerworlds.com/scifi

Sneak Peek

THE CURSE OF THE ARCADIAN STONE

She was solely created to guard a legendary relic. But when a rogue thief from Earth disrupts her dreary world, her job might not be the only thing she loses.

***

"What are you doing here?" He was giving me an odd look. "Are you lost?"

I pursed my lips. I really would have come off more credible if I were up in my tree.

"This place is dangerous." He waved me away. "You better get out of here."

I blinked. That was a switch. He was worried about *me*.

When I still didn't reply, he shrugged and turned to head in the direction of the Mystic Lake.

"Halt!" I stepped forward, raising my hand. "You mustn't go any further."

He stopped and turned back to look at me. "Halt...?"

I bit my tongue. I often forgot that languages evolved and that I had to adjust my manner of speaking. "I mean," I began again. "You must not go in that direction if you know what's good for you. If you are seeking the village, it is that way." I pointed in the other direction.

He looked up where I was pointing then back at me. "I've

just been to the village and trust me, babe, this direction is good for me."

I shot him a look of ridicule. *Babe?* I was over three thousand years old.

He continued to walk toward the Lake.

"Wait!" I went after him. "Please do not go any further. You must believe me. This is for your own safety." I tried to keep up with his long strides.

"Look babe, my safety is my business." His tone seemed firm, resolute.

"As the Guardian of this realm, it actually is my business," I declared. "And I am not a...*babe*." I made a face as I said it.

He paused and turned to me. "Oh, you're the guardian," he spoke as if in realization before his expression turned flat. "So?" he quipped and kept walking.

My serene smile faded when I saw that he was not about to cooperate. "Very well." I shrugged, finally spotting my tree and I drifted up to perch onto one of the lower branches as I watched him walk past below. "If you keep going, you will die," I called down to him. "No living creature can withstand the magical barrier around the Mystic Lake."

He stopped walking.

"Are you here for the relic?" I queried with a casual tone, leaning against the tree trunk.

"If that relic is a broken piece of glass, then it looks like I am."

He'd started to walk but stopped again when I went on. "No one who has ever tried to obtain the relic has survived these woods," I announced. "Trust me. It will do you no good to try to get it."

That made him look up at me, way up above him, and I felt my words sink in. I always did feel better up in my tree. The Forest was my territory. I smiled regally down at him.

"What's your name?"

I blinked again, surprised. "The last person who asked me that died too," I replied instead of answering. "He tried to reason about how badly he needed the relic. I'm afraid it does no good to explain to me. I can't help you," I relayed. "I can only warn you. Please leave while you can."

He gave me a critical look, studying me from head to toe before his eyes met mine again. "What's your name?" he repeated, his tone gentler.

"Um..." I was about to explain that I didn't really have a name but then reconsidered. "I was called—Magenta."

***

Enjoyed the preview?

Check out **The Curse of the Arcadian Stone: Nameless Fay** series books at your favorite online book store.

Other Titles by S. Breaker

S. R. BREAKER

Epic Fantasy series

The Secret of the Phoenix
The Curse of the Arcadian Stone: Nameless Fay

Fantasy Romance

Dragons of Arcadia Series
Arranged to the Fae Warrior (prequel)
Curse of the Dragon Heir
Reign of the Dragon Heir

SARA BREAKER

Sweet Romance

Holiday Blues
Change of Mind
Insert Happy Ending
Just an Alternate
Switch on Christmas
Crushing on You

Sneak Peek

CURSE OF THE DRAGON HEIR

A headstrong Fae mage accidentally sets a mysterious evil demon free but he may be the key to unlocking her powers...

***

"Are you mated yet?" His voice was gruff but deeply rich.

Soleia shot him a glare. "That's none of your business."

The three warrior females exchanged looks.

Oh, great, she thought in derision. Now they were probably going to start rumors about her and the demon. Just what she needed right now. "Thank you for your help." She dismissed the females with a wave before hanging up her cloak and turning back to fix her hair.

His scrutiny was unnerving her and also making her stomach do somersaults.

Stupid stomach. What the hell was wrong with her anyway? He was a cursed, dangerous demon that would destroy them all with one swish of his claws if given half the chance.

She cleared her throat, hurrying to finish grooming so she could exit the cramped indoor space, feeling a bit more cramped than before.

"Let me free."

Her eyebrows rose in incredulity at his words. "So you can kill me and everyone I know?"

He visibly swallowed hard. "I won't."

Soleia gave him a dull look. "Right."

His forehead creased in aggravation. "You don't even know who I am! How do you know it's justified to hold me against my will? How do you know you're not in the wrong here?"

"Look, the only wrong thing I did today was take too long at that dumb wraith forest. I should have ridden faster, fought harder. I should have just left some of the smaller wraiths alone. If I could have just put them to sleep, I could've—" She stopped short, blowing out a frustrated breath.

His eyes narrowed. "I thought you handled yourself quite well."

She gave him a deadpan look. "I know exactly what you're doing. You're trying to ply me with compliments so that I'll feel sorry for you or something and maybe release you from Oma's binding spell. But I'm not that dumb, Curse Boy."

He blinked like he didn't expect her to figure that out and he merely huffed in displeasure and looked away.

Soleia smirked. She was quite enjoying having so much power over him. "What kind of a dumb demon gets trapped on a tree anyway? And then to finally get free of the tree, only to get trapped by a necklace! Is this only the second curse that's been put on you? Or have there been more?"

That set him off.

He growled again, grabbing her by the shoulders and pinning her back against the wall.

She almost rolled her eyes at his futile intimidation efforts. Did he forget one word from her would send him doubling over? She met his gaze, undaunted. "You didn't scare me before. You definitely don't now."

He roared, leaning close to her face. He was clearly displeased, infuriated. "Mark my words," he rasped. "This spell *will* break. And when that time comes, I guarantee you, you *will* be scared. And then you will die."

"Right, whatever. But until then, Curse Boy, your life belongs to me." Soleia gave him a shove to push away but he pressed harder.

He was focused on her mouth. "Dathon," he growled. He spoke near her face. His freshly-showered scent was almost hypnotizing, overwhelming. Her chest heaved against his in her struggle to breathe and he must have noted her heart pounding. His incensed gaze seared into her. "My name is Dathon."

***

Enjoyed the preview? **Curse of the Dragon Heir** is also available to purchase at your favorite bookstore.